ALSO BY

LORENZA PIERI

The Garden of Monsters

LESSER ISLANDS

Lorenza Pieri

LESSER ISLANDS

*Translated from the Italian by
Peter DiGiovanni, William Greer,
Donatella Melucci, Jenna Menta,
Christopher Paniagua, and Kira Ross*

Europa
editions

Europa Editions
27 Union Square West, Suite 302
New York, NY 10003
www.europaeditions.com
info@europaeditions.com

Translation by Peter DiGiovanni, William Greer, Donatella Melucci,
Jenna Menta, Christopher Paniagua, and Kira Ross
Original title: *Isole minori*
Translation copyright © 2023 by Donatella Melucci

The translation of Isole minori *by Lorenza Pieri has been completed as a class
project by the students of Italian Translation (Fall 2020) taught by prof.
Donatella Melucci at Georgetown University. Their names are: Peter
DiGiovanni, William Greer, Jenna Menta, Christopher Paniagua,
and Kira Ross.
A former student of Italian Translation, Martina Benedetti Marshall,
proofread the manuscript along with prof. Melucci.
Prof. Melucci would like to acknowledge and thank all of them for their hard
work and dedication.*

Library of Congress Cataloging in Publication Data is available
ISBN 978-1-60945-825-6

Pieri, Lorenza
Lesser Islands

Art direction by Emanuele Ragnisco
instagram.com/emanueleragnisco

Prepress by Grafica Punto Print – Rome

Printed in Canada

CONTENTS

"What you thought was a tiny point on earth was all."
—ELSA MORANTE, *Arturo's Island*

LESSER ISLANDS

PART I
(1976 – 1977)

1.

We saw the dolphins in the morning. We trailed their shiny fins in the boat for a good half hour; then they went too far and Babbo, as people in Tuscany say Daddy, had to turn back. For me, it was the first time.

It was the end of August 1976. In general, the end of other people's vacations meant the beginning of ours. The tourists went back to their cities and while we waited patiently for autumn in a hot and long season, we had time and space to ourselves. Until the middle of October it was lows of 60°F and highs of 80°F, the sea was calm, and the beaches deserted. Only five kinds of noises could be heard: water against rocks, water against hulls, boat motors, screams of birds, and human voices. We had started going again on boat trips with Babbo, something we rarely did when the hotel was in full swing. At night he had friends over for dinner and sat them at the restaurant's open tables. Caterina and I would fill baskets with blackberries in the afternoon while we walked along the road to Cannelle.

That day, rather unusually, the air was heavy and humid with a coming sirocco. From the port, one could only just see the outline of Argentario, like a dinosaur surrounded by its sticky breath. When I got back from the boat trip, I told everyone that I had witnessed the stunning beauty of the dolphins. They looked at me with expressions of enthusiastic surprise, but I knew that they were only doing it to please me. I knew that seeing the dolphins in Giglio was not exactly an exceptional event. In the evening, I decided that I did not want to see fake expressions of surprise anymore. I would keep the magic for myself.

In any case, they were all concentrated on the *news*. The rumor was now official: Franco Freda and Giovanni Ventura, the two neofascist defendants accused of being the perpetrators of the Piazza Fontana massacre, would be sent into exile in Giglio a few days later. A fact that no one remembers today, that doesn't even appear in the most documented dossiers, in the chronological reconstructions of the process, or in the detailed books about the procedural issues regarding the Milan terrorist attack of 1969.

And yet, in those days, Freda and Ventura being sent into exile, along with the protests that followed, not only disrupted the calm of the island but also covered the front pages of the newspapers and inaugurated a new phase of the trial, which in the end produced the sole convicts from a case that closed after thirty-five years and without convinctions.

Seven years had passed since the bombing at the Agricultural Bank, with an array of arrests and subsequent releases, the premature deaths of twelve witnesses, the disappearance of evidence, three separate investigations, two governments, an attempted coup d'état, and two other massacres. The debt of the State in the pursuit of justice became suspiciously heavy.

The coordination of protests was unanimously assigned to our mother Elena. She was the most combative, the most knowledgeable, the one who brought a political consciousness to Giglio and took it upon herself to share it with whomever she could. Until '68, she lived in Bologna, where she served on the university student committees and belonged to the group that would later found the independent radio station Radio Alice. She studied economics, and, when she was twenty-four, started a doctorate on the Marxist concept of money as an alienated ability of mankind. Then she met Vittorio, my father, who was finishing veterinary school at twenty-seven years old, after spending the last couple of years wandering from one university to another in search of the easiest exams to pass. My mother helped him write his dissertation even though she had no knowledge of the topic ("Behavior Changes in Sport Horses Due to the Use of Bitless Bridles") and as soon as his dissertation defense was over they toasted with friends and left Bologna to vacation in Giglio. They arrived one evening in May, greeted by the scent of Scotch broom flowers. They had planned to stay two days, but they extended the vacation another five. When the day came to return, they had heard the owner of the hotel where they were staying, the San Lorenzo, say that he wanted to find new management so he could finally return to his family in Livorno, because none of his kids wanted to continue the business and he was tired of being there alone. My father, with the reckless instinct that guided his best actions, nominated himself as a candidate without even speaking to my mother. All he had to do was look outside from the salon window: the cliff of Gabbianara, the sea, a lemon tree full of fruit. Within three days they had signed the contract. A few weeks later, my mother discovered she was expecting a baby. She had returned to Bologna for a few days to organize the move of their humble belongings, and to every friend she greeted, she said, "I'm going to live on a small island and I'm pregnant; if it's a boy I will call him Arturo." The more disbelief she saw in their eyes, the happier she felt. She would remain in Giglio for twelve years.

She left behind the doctorate, the possibility of a scholarship to a German university, and her communist youth clubs to end up running a hotel and being a cook. She had discovered that she knew how to do it and took charge of a thankless task only because nobody else was doing it and she was incapable of standing back when something needed to be done. In the summer of '76 she was thirty-three years old. She had red hair and was tall, with a face and body covered in freckles and eyes of the burnt brown color that often accompanies fiery hair. She was a wild and untamed beauty. Someone had nicknamed her the Lioness, but in the end everyone called her Red because of her hair and, above all, her politics. Red was easier to fear than to love.

My father, who at the time was a boy and was not scared of anything, had chosen her more out of superficiality than anything else. The pain embedded in her eyes that had sent other boys running didn't scare Vittorio. Perhaps he had simply not been able to see it.

Red had called for a plenary meeting open to citizens and tourists on the porch of San Lorenzo at nine in the evening. She had closed the kitchens, suspended the dinner orders, reimbursed those who had full board, and arranged the chairs for the meeting. One person complained but the majority of the guests wanted to participate. She thought there would be about forty people at most, those from the city council and a few others interested in political matters, but instead, by eight forty-five, there were no more places to sit, not even on the tables stacked in the corner, and so they had to move outside. There were at least two hundred people there.

Caterina and I were zipping around the gathering on a bike together, me behind, standing with my hands resting on her shoulders. With us was Irma, the white-orange English setter that was the same age as Caterina and followed us everywhere. She was our bitch, as people said around here. Her real name was Immacolatella. It was my mother who chose both the puppy, the chubbiest one there was, and her name: since she had given birth to a little girl and could not name her Arturo, she thought to pay homage to Morante's novel with the name of the dog instead. But the name Immacolatella proved to be difficult and too long. When my sister started to speak, she called the puppy Imma and thus on my dad's suggestion she became Irma, like *Irma la Douce*, he had said.

Caterina and I didn't know exactly why all those adults were gathered there. We were too busy arguing about how to divide the two thousand lire that we had earned during the week at the stand where we sold handmade goods and old toys.

"Listen, I handmade all the paper diaries, I designed them, and I stapled them, and they're the things that made us money," Caterina said. "I should get at least a thousand and five because you didn't do anything."

"But that isn't true: I made the necklaces and the bracelets and the painted stones."

"We didn't sell your rocks."

"Yes we did, the one with the boat and the hedgehog sold."

"But those don't count because Babbo bought them so it isn't money earned. Anyways, you can have five hundred lire. Oh, that's a lot of money, eh?"

I was silent and she had the upper hand. We had spent a portion of the shared prize on gelato, and I had tapped my finger several times on the metal panel outside the bar saying, "I want this," and Caterina had told me, "Why are you yelling, you'll knock down the sign." We had gone to the café to get an ice-cream sandwich and a drumstick, and we stopped to eat them on the edge of the gathering of adults, at the center of which we weren't surprised to see our mother. Caterina listened to her and understood everything because even though she was only eight years old, she still felt perfectly comfortable with those who were twice her age, with whom she shared not only arguments but also adolescent rebellion.

I was there pretending to listen, shamelessly fixating on the feet of the old men sitting outside, their toes crossed in their flip-flops with those grey, curved, never cut, scary nails. The old men were eating ice cream with all the paper still wrapped around it, taking bites out of it without even licking, as if they weren't able to or as if sticking out their tongues was inappropriate behavior.

After a bit, I pulled Caterina by the sweater to make her move from there. On the pier, which we weren't venturing down by ourselves because it was too dark and dangerous to cross via bike, a group of boys was attaching banners to the lighthouse and someone, standing on the high wall, was watching the sea with a telescope and yelling something.

We observed them for a bit and then moved to the corner of the foosball table. There was a boy from Rome, Luigi, whom we knew well because his father Sergio was a drinking buddy of our father's. He and his wife were very rich and owned a villa at the Cannelle beach. They had nicknamed them "the Overkills" ever since, some years before, they had drunk so much at Luigi's baptism party that they forgot him at the bar, and it was the cleaning lady, apparently, who had delivered him home, sound asleep in his carrier. Rumor had it that she had debated whether or not to bring him directly to the Carabinieri.

We called him Luiggi, mimicking the way his mother Desideria said it. He had inserted a coin and turned the glass knob hard, and the balls had come down all together with the noise of an avalanche. Luiggi asked us if we wanted to play. I looked at Caterina; she had already turned away. "No. He cheats. Forget it." As he protested and swore to respect the rules, Caterina had again moved closer to the porch where the meeting was taking place. With a shrug of my shoulders, I said goodbye to the kid and followed her.

"This is an island where, until just a few years ago, people were starving. Our grandparents broke their backs to cultivate the vineyards, work the mines, and fish day and night. Tourism is a vital resource for us; it's not the enemy. If Giglio becomes a place of exile then nobody will visit anymore, just ask me. And then there are the prisons on Pianosa and Capraia. This archipelago can't be transformed into a prison on the sea!" Beppe was speaking, also known as Bazza, a nickname which, like those of many other islanders, had been passed down through generations, and in this case was additionally justified by a chin that had also been inherited from father to son.

Sitting on the edge of a table, Mario, known as Cuore, raised his voice.

"It's notttt! This isn't about protecting tourism and the image of the island—it seems like money is all that matters to you. There's something more serious going on: the Italian justice system is protecting criminals, there's a dangerous State project behind this. They're sending them here because it makes it easier for them to escape, because they want them to get away, don't you see? Why else, after four years of house arrest, would they not give him a proper trial? Because here there are people, without naming names, who would welcome Almirante and any other fascist into their homes. And guys, let's be clear, they're sending them here because from Giglio, Corsica is only a few hours away by motorboat. It's as simple as that. The secret service organize everything for them just like they did for Giannettini. He was up to his neck in it and now he lives a good life in the Côte D'Azur. All paid for by the government of course. And why do you think they chose Giglio and not Elba, for example? Or Ponza? Because here, my dears, we're all Christian Democrats."

People stirred in the back. The crowd had naturally arranged itself into small groups by party, and the Christian Democrats were all together. The old women who participated from their balconies facing the street leaned forward to hear better. Voices rose and crossed over one another.

"Oh Mario, now what the fuck does it matter that we're all Christian Democrats? Today the city council met in a special session and agreed that they shouldn't be allowed to come."

"Eh, good Kissinger! So what are you waiting for? If we don't want them to come we need to organize something, because Ventura will arrive tomorrow: tonight he'll already be in Grosseto and tomorrow morning they'll embark."

Antonio, the bartender with a hole in his chin like a fingerprint in dough, turned toward a tourist couple sitting next to him: "The Christian Democrats can't just use this island however they please, to send whomever they want on a nice vacation instead of jail."

Someone interrupted him.

"Antonio, if you have something to complain about, raise your voice and say it to our faces."

"No, nothing. I was just explaining to the foreign lady that thirteen of the sixteen council members here are from the CD . . ."

"And what's wrong with that? Right now we have to decide what to do so that Freda and Ventura don't come. Let's not get off track."

Gigi the Hoarse raised his voice, scratched by cigars and nights at sea: "They say that Valpreda has been hospitalized in Brindisi and won't come. Kidney stones. But then someone saw him at the bar having a Campari."

Paola Muri had turned twenty that summer and was a young friend of my parents. She was from Milan, even though she was half Gigliese, and had a response for almost any question. She stood up and all of a sudden her curls came loose, came so loose that she looked almost scary, Medusa-like. She was horrified, and she screamed because she hadn't yet learned how to be diplomatic and held her beliefs so strongly that it seemed impossible to her that not everyone agreed with them.

"There it is, exactly what they wanted. Confusing Freda with Valpreda, one a murderer and the other an innocent man! The person who was hospitalized, Ventura's companion, the one who's coming here for exile, is Franco Freda, FRE-DA, NOT VAL-PRE-DA! Valpreda is the anarchist unjustly implicated in the massacre. He also did three years in prison awaiting trial, despite there not being a shred of evidence against him, and he has yet to be fully acquitted. Freda, on the other hand, was charged with evidence; *he* was the one who bought the timers that set off the bombs. Everybody knows it. He had an arsenal of weapons at Castelfranco Veneto. And he was already in jail for having organized other train attacks. Valpreda is not Freda! And this confusion is unbearable, it's a double injustice!"

Gigi the Hoarse lowered his head, a bit intimidated, assuming a pose that didn't suit his powerful physique or his wooden and sun-browned face, which somehow still managed to redden. He tried in vain to whisper that it wasn't his fault that their names all sounded the same. His embarrassment made everyone embarrassed, because nobody was used to seeing an old man chewed out by a young woman.

Angiolino nudged Gigi with a chuckle: "You always butt in like a fool! Next time you better shut up!"

Red, who knew well the somewhat ignorant elderly and how humiliating a situation like that was for them, helped Gigi divert the attention from himself, guiding the conversation away from Paola's indignation and toward the government, a target that was not present at their outdoor meeting.

"It's a shame that they did all that just to erase evidence. The Carabinieri even blew up the briefcase with the only bomb that remained intact. It could have been a decisive piece of evidence. But it will be clear that the government is directly involved if justice swings that way. Seven years have passed since Piazza Fontana, not one. And they have yet to hold a single trial. They used all their methods of distraction to protect the powerful: obstruction, state secrets, hijacking of trials. If it's not the government behind all of this . . ."

"It's obvious," Ettore reaffirmed.

But Elena the Red hadn't finished. It was late and she had to put her daughters to bed. She needed to say her piece now.

"Saragat, who has made agreements with the Americans, is probably also involved. Do you remember when Nixon came to Rome in '69? What did he come to do? He was worried that Italy would be drawn into the orbit of the Soviets, and so they agreed to engage in a strategy of rising tensions. A delightful period of attacks to justify an authoritarian government, which was by that point legitimized . . ."

Mario interrupted again: "Yes, it's a shame that so many people know these things that you know, but there's no way to prove them. And in the meantime after seven years there's not even a culprit."

Elena sat up, said something in her husband's ear and inched her chair away from his. Then she turned to Mario and Ettore, who were in the same corner, ignoring the others. Her non-Tuscan accent betrayed a difference, a lack of belonging, that she tried to make up for ideologically.

"Then it seems to me that in one way or another we are almost all in agreement. We don't let Freda and Ventura land. We'll meet tomorrow morning on the dock at about half past seven; whoever doesn't want to do it just let me know. I'm sorry, but I have to go now."

She gave a quick wave goodbye, and as she raised her thin wrist the many bone bracelets she wore fell towards her elbow. Before coming to collect us, she trained her dark eyes on Gullo, who was eighteen: she was sure that the next day he wouldn't be missing. There was a moment of silence as everyone watched her tall figure in the floral skirt disappear around the corner of the porch. The meeting dissolved into confused chatter.

2.

Sitting on the bed in short-sleeved pajamas that differed from mine only in size and color (in my opinion, hers were much more beautiful), Caterina was reading me a bedtime story from the magic book. I wanted her to read me the same one as yesterday, the one about the pufferfish that put everyone to sleep when it spoke; but Caterina explained to me that it was impossible, that the book was magic precisely because every night there was a new story, and those that had already been read disappeared off the page. I still hardly knew how to read: I would start first grade a few weeks later, whereas Caterina was about to go into fifth. She had skipped kindergarten and finished two years in one, so she ended up two grades ahead by the end of elementary school. She had already read the entire encyclopedia of animals to me, which became my fixation.

The magic book didn't have any illustrations and the words were very small. On the white hardcover was nothing but mysterious barbed wire. In reality, it was probably a book about the Holocaust or some other tragedy from twentieth-century concentration camps, but Caterina just pretended to read and invented a new story for me every night and even if I knew it, I still enjoyed the moment. If I wasn't naïve, I was acting naïve. It was a great pleasure I felt, giving Caterina the satisfaction of commanding and manipulating me. I blindly trusted her: it felt totally without risk.

"Now I'm going to read you a story that Mom once read to me. *Once upon a time, in a faraway land, there was a very bad king. The king made everyone work and pay taxes, and with his wealth he threw big parties to which he only invited his three monster friends: one blue, very clever; one black, very strong; and one green, very normal. One day a group of his younger subjects, the red boys, decided to rebel, and they began to disrespect the king. They threw rotten prickly pears at his carriage, wrote on the walls with permanent markers, and stole the pine cones hanging from the cuckoo clock. The king wanted to make them stop. So, he asked the blue monster, the clever one, for advice. The blue monster had an idea and the king followed his advice. He waited until Wednesday when all his subjects were in the square for the market and had the black monster throw an enormous rock right into the middle of the fountain. The fountain split apart and the people got all wet; some got hit in the head with pieces of it while others had their groceries fly away, pears rolling every which way. Everyone was furious and wanted to know who had done it? Own up now, and pay us back for our groceries! Nobody came forward. Then the king said that the red boys did it, and the people said enough, these kids have to stop! The king was very pleased that he could have them arrested. This had been the blue monster's plan and it looked like it was about to work. But as it turned out the green monster eventually said, no, look, I saw the black monster throw the rock. The black monster said, who, me? Certainly not! The king said, who, him? Certainly not! The green monster said, but I saw you; the black monster said, you're wrong; the king said, you're wrong; the people said, we want to know who did it; the black monster said in the king's ear, look, you're the one who told me to throw the rock, now please save me; and so they wasted a lot of time. The people said, enough, the black monster should go to jail. The king didn't know what to do, but he made a decision: we'll send the black monster far away to a small island where nobody will recognize him, and this way he will be fine and the people will be satisfied. And, in fact, after a long journey, the black monster is arriving in Giglio tomorrow. The end."*

"But Cate, the black monster doesn't really exist," I pointed out at the end of the reading.

"Of course he exists and he's arriving soon. His name is Fredevventura."

"But that's not true, this is a fairy tale."

"Yes, it is true. Fredevventura has two heads, four arms, and four legs. He's like a giant spider, but when you look at him, he transforms into a man."

"You're a liar."

"I'm telling you the truth. Why do you think those strong boys were on the dock tonight? Did you notice they had binoculars? They're watching to see if Fredevventura will arrive tonight. Come look. Didn't you hear Mom and Dad talking about it?"

Caterina got out of bed and dragged me to the window. From our room, we could see the harbor.

"What did I tell you? Can't you see they're all there? You don't need to be scared—the boys won't let him come. Let's go to bed now.

We went to bed. After the light had been off for a bit, I slipped into Caterina's bed, in silence, and snuggled up very close to her side, putting her hair in my mouth like I always did. Caterina did not protest and we fell asleep stuck together like two spoons in the cutlery drawer.

3.

My mother woke very early and put on a pair of pants from a pile of clothes on a chair and a clean blue and white striped shirt. She said goodbye in a rush and left without her purse, as she often did, because she never really needed it. The purse was useful for me, though, to rifle through, getting my nails dirty with the kohl that was smeared on the bottom of it while searching for butterscotch candies with their wrappings all stained and sandy.

She tried not to slam the door, but after three failed attempts she gave it the hard hit that was the only way to make it close.

Mom went down the alley, where she encountered a smell that mixed cats with the recently retired ladies of the night and the coffee that was starting to snake out from open windows. With her toes pressed against the tips of her clogs, trying in vain to slow the natural acceleration of the seaward slope, it took her two minutes to get to the harbor. She immediately ran into Ettore. He was a sailor who sometimes worked on ferries but more often on long-distance cargo ships. He alternated months of sailing with periods of rest, and when he returned home in his off months he dedicated himself to politics. Time had transformed the way he looked, but ever since I'd been a baby I saw him as a strong and just giant, like the workers in images of the Russian Revolution. He had broad and square shoulders, a long mustache, and a shirt that always only had two buttons done up. He rarely smiled. The furrows between his eyebrows were quick to appear, like those of a worried person. He was affectionate with me and Caterina and had played a significant role in our learning how to swim when we were very young.

"Well?" Elena asked him.

"I stayed up all night, but I didn't see anything. At one point someone arrived on a motorboat. We asked him for his documents, he was a reporter from the *Messaggero*. He got drunk on two glasses of wine and is asleep in my house. At seven we called the Porto Santo Stefano and warned them not to let the *Rio Marina* depart, which was useless. They replied that it would leave no matter what, and that the Carabinieri had already been alerted. Authorities from Giglio are here and have already reported our names to the Orbetello police department."

"But at this time the ferry should already be visible, no?" It was a little after eight.

"Eh, sure, but look at the fog," said Ettore, pointing to the sea. The horizon was so milky and dense that it merged sea and sky into a sheet of opaque metal. Elena left and went all the way to the entrance of the church, taking the steps two by two. She thought that if God existed He would have taken that façade with its blind arches as a gesture of little respect towards Him. But quickly she regained her focus. From her elevated vantage point she pointed her gaze as far toward the horizon as she could. Then she ran back and grabbed Ettore by his open shirt: "Quick, we need a blockade, right away. The ferry will be here in half an hour." He had already procured one of the long, thick ropes that were used for securing tankers. He fastened the initial noose to the ring of the cleat, then jumped quickly from one boat to another, finally reaching his small wooden boat. Red was waiting for him on the dock. A small crowd had gathered around her. Ettore reached them with three vigorous strokes of his paddle, people passed him the rope over the bow, and she took off her wooden clogs and climbed aboard. He pushed off with the boat hook, and the boat started to move with the force of his shove while the cable began to unravel into the sea. The oars cut rhythmically through the clear surface of the water. In a minute they made it to the other side. Ettore threw the advance line to the dock, and the rope stretched just above the water between the two lighthouses. It was 8:15 A.M., the ferry was now visible offshore and the port barred by an obstacle that was too precarious. The rope would not be enough. Rolling up the hem of her pants so as not to get soaked, Elena said to him, "Let's row out to the middle. If the ferry wants to pass, it will have to run over us."

He nodded and moved the boat to the exact center of the harbor. On the lighthouse were hung two sheets that said in red letters from the same hand: "FASCIST MURDERERS. Seven years to wait for JUSTICE are too many" and "GIGLIO

IS HONEST—FASCISTS TO PRISON NOW." By then the port was packed with people, and it was strange: there hadn't been this many people even at the procession of the Madonna Stella Maris. Nevertheless there was an overwhelming silence.

The tourists that had tickets for the 8:50 ferry arrived on the dock. Seeing that there was no hope of leaving, they parked the vans, the Renault 4 and the Fiat 127, packed to the gills with bags and inflatable rafts on their roofs.

The line of cars was joined by a line of boats that were equally confused and began to crowd the mouth of the harbor. In less than twenty minutes a flotilla had blocked access to the harbor. Fourteen wooden boats, two inflatable rafts, two motorboats, a sailboat moored sideways, a fishing boat, and three little launches. They closed ranks by squeezing their bumpers up against one another and creating a barricade united by a single mooring from one dock to another. People started to climb aboard the floating blockade holding the banners: "THERE'S NO PLACE FOR CRIMINALS HERE" was hoisted to the main mast of the sailboat. Paola had made the sign, soaking her toes and heels in the red paint to make footprints, and standing there, barefoot, she looked like she was bleeding. Another sign was strung between two boats, made from a single sheet with a faded flower print: "INCARCERATION NOT VACATION FOR FREDA AND VENTURA." By now the ferry had reached the harbor. For more than twenty minutes it slowly bobbed in place, moving neither backwards nor forward, listing slightly to the side, as if drawn by a child, emitting a low and deafening note that was audible from every point on the island. From where Elena stood, aboard the wooden launch that was precisely centered in the barricade, the prow of the ferry was much more than a sad beast: it was like an armored vehicle that, if it had continued forward, would have smashed through all the vessels it came in contact with without a problem, and, wrecking hulls and shredding ropes, would have sunk that improvised maritime battalion in just a few minutes. Instead, it kept on resolutely with the siren blows. The people on the boats covered their ears with their hands; some raised their oars vertically and brandished them like rifles, making the barricade more visible. This lasted less than an hour but seemed much longer to everyone; then the ferry began its slow turn. With the stern facing port, the boat turned back with its load of tourists and terrorists, creating a white whirlpool in the water that foamed with rage.

Applause exploded from the marine trench and spread over the crowded wharves. Someone had brought something to drink and the bottles were passed from boat to boat and from mouth to mouth even though it was early in the morning.

In that very instant of collective exaltation, my sister and I arrived with our father. He had loaded us on a rolling cart that he usually used to move boxes of linen and food from the ferry to the hotel; for us that day it was a rickshaw.

He was stopped by the marshal of the Carabinieri. He let the handles go and made us get down, and we began applauding like the others without knowing why. In Giglio there were three Carabinieri in total, and they had seen more regattas than roundups. During the winter, they let the people of Giglio regulate themselves, trying to integrate with the locals as best they could while knowing that they would always remain outsiders anyway. There were no infractions to be sanctioned nor regulations to be made. When they had to report on their work to management they made things up. The patrol officer went to bars, to the pharmacy, to the outpatient clinic, and asked, "Boys, shall we write some tickets?" The citizens who were most generous or had the biggest sense of guilt volunteered for the false fines and parking tickets that had gone ignored for years, paying a one-time fee that sealed a non-aggression pact for good. Vittorio was a great supporter of that practice. That was the price of anarchy for the majority of the year: some sporadic and completely arbitrary punishment. He enjoyed telling friends who came from afar, about this regime of freedom. Because certainly in the summer things changed a bit. When the tourists arrived, the Carabinieri had to give parking tickets, search the backpacks of the hippies for drugs, break up drunk fights, verify that no free camping happened and that fires weren't lit on the beaches, and file accident reports. And now, just as summer was coming to an end, this giant problem had reared its head. The marshal said to my father, "Sir, someone called from Grosseto: the chief of police will arrive by helicopter today. You know that to block the harbor is a serious crime, right? We had to give them names, because they'll inevitably press charges. If you all stop the protest maybe everything ends here, but sending the ferry back was a big mistake. You know your lady is on the boat in the middle, right?" At the words "your lady," Vittorio felt a pang of annoyance. "What do you want me to say? Do what you have to do and we will, too." He left the marshal and the cart next to a bench and headed toward the lighthouse. We meanwhile had run in the opposite direction to see who was on the boats. The islanders were all at the protest and the tourists who weren't among them protested that they couldn't leave or have breakfast because the bartender was at the protest, too. He had closed the bar with a turn of the key, leaving a note that said "I'll be back when I've finished." We cut the line at the ferry ticket kiosk. We made it to the green lighthouse. Caterina yelled, "Look, there's Mom, in the middle!" I couldn't see her. "Where? Where? Let's go!" and I started to get on the first boat in the row, leaning out with my hand still in hers, my foot reaching through the air and my ass hovering over the water. Caterina held me back with all the strength she could muster: "Where are you going, you crazy thing? You'll fall into the sea."

Evidently, we must have screamed very loudly or our mother had an ear that was attuned to our voices, because she turned immediately around from her small boat and motioned to us not to move. She said something to Ettore and slowly climbed the bridge of boats, moving with caution, holding her flip-flops in one hand and giving the other to whomever helped her across. She was moving her body timidly, as if her never-combed red hair and large breasts that hadn't nursed me, all of that out-of-control beauty, were out of proportion on her, as if she had never gotten accustomed to them.

"Who brought you two here?"

"We came with Babbo," Caterina replied defensively.

"And now where is he?" I looked at the ground in a guilty silence as if in the euphoria of the party we had lost him. Caterina was ready: "The Carabinieri stopped him."

"You're coming home with me now and staying there." She took us by the hand and we made our way through the crowd.

"What happened, Mom?" Caterina asked.

"It's complicated. Nothing that concerns you, anyway," she replied in an annoyed tone, looking back at her friends still at sea.

"It's for Fredevventura, isn't it?" Caterina continued, to no reply. I was sure that during the night they had rescheduled the feast of that day's patron saint and now Mom was angry because we had lost Babbo and she didn't want us participating in what was happening. About a month and a half prior, at the procession for San Lorenzo, I, like all the other younger kids, had walked in the parade dressed like a sailor, with golden braids and a square collar with a trim of tiny stars that hung on my back. The older children, however, were dressed as little angels with bright satin pleats, cardboard wings, crowns made out of pine garlands, and baskets full of petals to be scattered along the ground before the saint passed by. I had deeply envied my sister's pink cherub costume and her role as a rose-scatterer. I had broken ranks before the end of the parade when I saw my friend Pietro, my only male playmate, waving me over to watch the regatta from the terrace of his house.

Now Mom was taking us home, but not before I had glimpsed the regatta boats and heard the applause. I tried again. "Mom, is the regatta happening now?" She laughed and Caterina said to me, "You are so stupid." My mother gave her a slap.

"Mom, can you take them to Cannelle?" Elena yelled as she entered the house through the door that was always open. Nonna Alina, Nonnalina to us, was in the kitchen with the radio on and didn't respond.

While we waited for the construction of our new house to be completed, the five of us lived in a seven hundred and fifty square foot rental home with a kitchen, bathroom, double bedroom, another bedroom with two beds against the same wall, one in front of the other like train wagons, living room, kitchen and no view of the sea surrounding the home, which made it a masterpiece of architectural perversion. Nonnalina slept in the living room on a cot which during the day was folded in two and hidden behind the window curtain. But she never complained. She still managed to find her own corner in our room: she had her own wardrobe and a chest of drawers to herself, on which rested photos of her loved ones and a jewelry box without any jewels inside. Now and then Elena and Vittorio spent the night in a room at the San Lorenzo. In the summer, though, the hotel was all full, and in the winter the heaters were not turned on for a single room.

Nonnalina was my mother's only family. She came from a small village in Romagna and was staying with us because

Elena needed her and vice versa. She had been widowed at twenty-six years old, right after the war, with a newborn daughter and a house in the countryside that was half crumbled to the ground from bombings. She had rearranged her maimed destiny into a new cell, mother–daughter. She started from nothing. An absolute zero: no home, no work, no education, no husband. And an unbearable tragedy that had taken him away from her and was never to be discussed.

Nonnalina had found herself, in an era that was still well before the feminist revolution, a young mother and semi-illiterate worker, sharing a basement apartment in the city with another widow. The government, to repay her on behalf of her martyred husband, gave her a gold medal and a job as a cashier in the municipal public baths, which in the postwar period were still elegant, warm, familiar, and very popular. I always asked my nonna to tell me stories about the baths, about all the people that had to go to wash themselves outside because they didn't have showers or tubs at home, about Mom, who in her childhood had slept on couches of red velvet in the waiting room while Nonnalina worked, and about her colleague, Emilia, whom she called Miglia. Miglia was also a widow and victim of multiple misfortunes: the murder of her twelve-year-old son at the hands of the fascists; the suicide of her second son with polio, who had thrown himself under a train; her violent and alcoholic husband, who had pushed her out of the window, leaving her forever disabled and who died prematurely, thankfully, of cirrhosis of the liver. Miglia always sang while she cleaned toilets and tubs. While Nonnalina gave change back without missing a beat, she who had made it only through the third grade, Miglia now and then entered the baths with some gentleman "to wash his back" and rounded the price up with a tip proportionate to the wash. Miglia and Nonnalina were different but the best of friends, so much so that when Miglia passed away Nonnalina inherited her earrings, two round drops of obsidian with a tiny pearl in the center, that she wore for years without ever taking them off. For Nonnalina the only way to redeem herself was to make her daughter study, and not send her to work at the age of fourteen, convinced that eliminating the ignorance in which she herself had remained entrapped was the only way she could really change things.

When Caterina and I were born, Nonnalina retired to be with and help Elena. We were a strange female fruit tree, transplanted from the Po Valley to the island where my father had woven his comfortable spider's web, almost unintentionally, waited upon and revered as the only man in the family and as such always watched and criticized, too. We were all women, but perhaps I was the only one to notice it, even quite early on. The others, forced into independence, grew accustomed to filling a wider role, to not seek help from a man, to never evade a responsibility, to never, under any circumstances, use an alleged weakness to obtain something. They had lived as men, with male attitudes. Only I was aware of the power of being a sweet girl, a baby girl. And as long as I was able, up until my adolescence, I practiced it on my father but also on the other women of the family. Except then I almost always found myself in the position of the natural subaltern. "Shut up, what do you know?" was the response to my rare interjections. At the time it felt comfortable and right. It came to seem more and more convenient, but I had not yet understood that the world rests in the hands of men, those whom nobody can shut up.

It wasn't even ten in the morning but something was already frying in the pan.

Nonna asked in her dialect what had happened and if the fascists had arrived.

"No, we blocked the ferry and there may have only been Ventura, because Freda pretended to have kidney dysfunction and is still in the hospital at Brindisi. Take the kids to the sea or go for a walk, but don't come to the port. It's a total disaster there."

Caterina objected. "But I don't want to go to the sea with Nonna—the weather is bad today and I want to come to the protest, I want to stay on the boats with you."

"No, Caterina, you can't."

"But why not? Everyone is there, I want to be there too."

I interrupted: "C'mon, Cate, what does it matter, let's dig for sea worms on the beach."

"Shut up, what do I care about finding sea worms? Today they're staging a revolution and I'm supposed to go dig holes in the sand?"

My mother was already at the door, with Caterina right behind.

"Well if Cate comes I want to go too: it's not fair to just bring her."

"Teresa is right. So both of you stay here."

Caterina started one of her temper-tantrum cries. She hated crying in front of others, but her anger and shame were so strong that she couldn't hold back tears. In fact, she cried with disconcerting ease, like a small baby, despite her incredible maturity.

Nonna intervened. She ignored everything else and turned to mother: "But will you not be back for lunch? *Oja da parparé par tot?*" Should I make enough for everyone? A very difficult life, that of Nonnalina, full of sacrifices and renunciations, enormous pains, and yet they were all punctuated by the quotidian concerns that seemed to be the most difficult things to confront: the timings of lunch and dinner, how many people to feed, the right portions and sufficient cleaning, as if the purpose of every day were to prove that even in this overcrowded house nothing had ever been used, wasted, or out of place, as if removing all traces of life were the point of life itself. It was her salvation, probably. Those gestures contained all her worldly being, the worries the sense of her existence: to do something good, every day, to provide for others without expecting any thanks or recognition, an automatic duty, to be accomplished without being asked, without expecting any paradise.

My parents did not return for lunch. We ate with Nonna in the silence of the kitchen full of intimacy and well-established rituals. My sister did not speak to me for the entire afternoon. After lunch she went into my parents' room and began to play alone with her drawings, as she did almost every day. She would design a character, a girl usually, and then other figures around her, depending on the story that she invented, which she sometimes carried on for days, adding details, characters, and plot twists. The story was told only through the dialogue that she portrayed and mimicked while she drew. There were never children in her drawings. She was an illustrator, a playwright, and an actress at only eight and a half years old, but nobody in my house noticed; it was one of the ways she spent her time, just like any other. Only Nonnalina thought it an abnormal thing; after hearing Caterina talking to herself in front of a sheet of paper for hours she would tell her to stop, considering the game to be a sign of some mental illness, rather than one of precocious and exceptional creativity.

I went into the living room and since I was alone I took the record that had two planets on the cover and I looked first on one side and then on the other for that song that you weren't supposed to listen to because it said *they saw you lift your skirt up to your hair*, and, at a certain point, it even said *whore*, and I imagined that this girl drank at a fountain, pulling up her skirt with her hands so as to not get herself wet and underneath she wasn't wearing underwear. I listened to it secretly, learned it by heart,

and one time I sang it at dinner with some family friends who had
given me sparkling wine, and everyone was dying laughing and
wanted me to sing it at every dinner from then on. My mother
glared at anyone who tried to ask me to do it. Among those who
requested it was usually also my father, Vittorio.

Suddenly Caterina arrived and startled me. "What are you
doing?"

I detached the thumbtack from the record and made it
screech.

"What are you listening to?"

"The one called, 'Com'è profondo il mare.'"

"Yeah right, I know which one you're listening to."

I blushed. I saw that on the table were the curtain rods that
held up the synthetic curtains of the French door that Nonna
had washed. I grabbed one to change the subject. "Should we
play musketeers?"

Caterina took the other rod and quickly stabbed me in the
stomach. They were very sharp since they had to drive into the
window jamb.

"Hit! Wounded! Dead!"

"No, c'mon, that doesn't count, we hadn't even started."

We started playing again, and suddenly I made a jab that hit
her face. Caterina threw her rod on the ground, covered her
face with her hands, and started to yell. Between her fingers I
thought I saw blood. I was immobilized, unable to formulate
words. Nonnalina arrived immediately and her presence only
increased my terror that something serious had happened. She
also started to scream in dialect: "Oh my God, Holy Mary,
what happened?"

Caterina cried louder still: "You blinded me, you blinded
me, help!" I was terrified. I was sure that I would have to live
my whole life by her side, the guilty companion of a mon-
strous young girl with a glass eye and a black eye patch like a
pirate. Nonnalina, grabbing me by the arm, ordered me to run

to the harbor and look for Mom and Babbo. From that trip I remember only the terror that moved my legs, the screams of Nonnalina echoing behind me, and Irma chasing me with her tongue hanging out and me, flying, as if she were hunting me. I knew exactly where to find my mother.

By now it was late afternoon but the protest was still going, the harbor blocked off, tourists and Gigliesi assembled between the piers. The news that my sister had lost an eye took only a moment to make its way across the island.

My mother was gathering telegrams and a poster from the Proletarian Democratic Party, which had traveled from Grosseto to Porto Santo Stefano and finally arrived to Giglio by fishing boat, and she was hanging them on the walls of the porch at the restaurant, which had become the headquarters of the protest.

I almost broke the glass door as I came in. I couldn't manage to speak but she immediately knew that something had happened to Caterina.

We ran towards the house, elbowing through the crowd that was curiously observing the reaction of someone in the midst of a tragedy. Mom sent someone to call a doctor and another person to search for my father. When we arrived at the house Caterina was lying on the kitchen table and Nonna was holding her head. I was out of breath but I held it nevertheless. I passed out.

Caterina had just a small cut right on the arch of her eyebrow and Nonna had positioned her so that the wound would bleed less and she could see where to apply the hydrogen peroxide and the Band-Aid. When the doctor arrived, he was more useful to me than to my sister. Next came screams to relieve the tension, accusations and apologies, an impromptu session of child psychoanalysis mediated by the doctor, Caterina's reproaches to my mother that she should have brought her along to the harbor, and my apologies, which received in reply a grim look from my sister and a forefinger pointing towards her wounded eye. But apart from Caterina's sulking, I was not punished in any way. Not even a talking to. The fact was that I'd confessed, asked out loud to be forgiven, said that I would never aim for the eyes again. But nobody listened to me. It was obvious that I hadn't done it on purpose. In truth, I had seen exactly where my blow would land before extending my elbow. But surely everyone else was right. I accepted my innocence: I didn't count for anything, even when it came to justified punishment.

By the time my father arrived, the drama had already shrunk to a tiny Band-Aid on her eyebrow and red eyes. He asked my sister to explain what had happened to her, as she sat curled up and wrapped in a blanket on the couch in front of the Brionvega TV, with the air of a serious convalescent. He asked her to raise her head and she did; he then slowly removed the Band-Aid and told her that he had to look at it.

"Oh my! It's much more serious than I thought," he said, squinting his eyes.

She, who until that moment had been staring at the television, turned to scrutinize his expression.

"Ah yes my dear, I actually should give you two stitches."

"What did you say?"

"Well, yes, it's not a big deal. I recently sewed shut the belly of a dog, there's a bit of thread left, I can suture the wound. It's deep enough."

Caterina stood up. "Don't you dare!"

He left the room and returned with a leather briefcase that contained his veterinary instruments. He placed it on the table and pulled out a long curved needle from which hung a thick black thread. "Lie down on the table," he said.

Caterina ran screaming for Mom who was in her bedroom. They returned to the living room together, Caterina crying.

"You're a cry baby, you can't even take a joke," my father said.

"Vittorio," intervened my mother, "you always have to make a joke out of it, minimize everything, make fun of people. Don't you ever try to put yourself in someone else's shoes? Try to understand how a little girl, who could have lost an eye and is now being chased with a needle and thread to be sewn up like a dog, would feel?"

My father raised his voice. He swore. "Almost lost an eye? She has a tiny scratch—almost lost an eye my ass. It wasn't even close; you are so dramatic and you're turning her into you! You have to take everything so seriously, everything! You never let yourself laugh at anything, you turn every joke into a tragedy."

And turning his back to Caterina and Mom, Babbo grabbed me by the waist and lifted me on one shoulder. "Come on, you, I'll operate on you since nobody listens to me." He set me on the table and made me lie down. He held down my wrists with his hands. His face was over mine.

"Mmm, here we need a little anesthesia." He closed his mouth and dangled a bit of saliva from his lips over my face. I tried to wriggle away, screaming and laughing. "Helppppp, Dad's spitting on meeeeee."

Caterina came in the kitchen and looked at us, disgusted. Then she said, "I so badly want a normal father, with a mustache, who comes home in the evening and instead of making idiotic jokes says to me, *Good evening Caterina, how was your day?*"

That childhood desire would forever hold a certain sway in my sister's life, leading her to develop a certain propensity toward serious men, shady ones, near-sociopaths. In short, the opposite of my father.

From that evening on, whenever he greeted Caterina he would speak in a fake baritone, putting on a somber air and say, "Good evening Miss Caterina, did you have a good day today?" She would shake her head and pretend to ignore him, then throw herself onto her sheets of paper to draw.

4.

A few mornings later, Caterina was reading aloud the telegrams pinned to the walls of our restaurant.

"NO PLACE BESIDES A PRISON SHOULD HOST FASCIST MURDERERS I EXPRESS MY SOLIDARITY AND THAT OF THE TUSCAN SOCIALISTS FOR THE LEGITIMATE ACTION BY THE PEOPLE OF GIGLIO TO PREVENT THE ARRIVAL OF FREDA AND VENTURA EXECUTIVE COMMITTEE TUSCAN REGION ISP."

"I EXPRESS MY FULL SOLIDARITY FOR THE ACTION BY THE POPULATION OF THE ISLAND OF GIGLIO AIMED AT PREVENTING THE ARRIVAL OF FASCIST MURDERERS DIRECTOR ITALIAN ISP."

"But what does es-pee-i mean?" I asked.

"Es pee i is the acronym that stands for the Italian Socialist Party, they're the ones from the fairy tale, remember?"

"Oh, right."

"'Oh, right' what?" my sister challenged me. "Let's hear what you understood."

"They were the, the . . . the red boys."

"And who would they be?"

"The ones who you said were teasing the king, who were throwing rotten figs . . . ?"

"Yes, okay. And what are these telegrams saying?"

"Not sure."

"Okay. You don't understand anything. Let's move along, we'll see if there are better ones."

"WORKERS, COMRADES, THE FREEING OF FREDA AND VENTURA AND THEIR EXILE ON THE ISLAND

OF GIGLIO IS YET ANOTHER CONFIRMATION OF THE COMPLICITY OF THE AUTHORITIES OF THE CHRISTIAN-DEMOCRATIC REGIME WITH THE FAS-CISTS WHO FOR SEVEN YEARS HAVE BEEN BLOOD-YING ITALY WITH MASSACRES AND MURDERS.

"FOR ALL THIS TIME, THE JUDICIARY HAS NOT 'BEEN ABLE' TO CONDEMN TO LIFE IMPRISON-MENT THOSE WHO BY NOW EVERYONE KNOWS WERE THE ORGANIZERS OF THE MASSACRE AT PIAZZA FONTANA. THE RESOLUTE PROTEST BY THE INHABITANTS OF THE ISLAND OF GIGLIO THAT ALL SINCERE DEMOCRATS FOLLOW WITH SYMPA-THY INDICATES THE WILL OF THE POPULAR MASSES TO NOT GIVE RESPITE TO THE FASCIST MURDERERS AND TO THROW THEM BACK IN THE JAILS THAT ARE THE ONLY PLACE FIT FOR THEM. THE KILLER VENTURA IS NOW AT GROSSETO, GUEST OF THE HOTEL ORENA, PROTECTED BY THE POLICE AND BY LOCAL FASCISTS. THE WORKERS AND THE ANTIFASCISTS OF GROSSETO, IN SOLI-DARITY WITH THOSE LIVING ON GIGLIO, DEMAND THAT VENTURA DOES NOT STAY FOR EVEN ONE HOUR LONGER IN OUR PROVINCE. THUS, WE INVITE THE LOCAL AUTHORITIES, THE LEFT-WING PARTIES, THE UNIONS TO TAKE A FIRM STANCE AND MOBILIZE AGAINST THE PRESENCE OF VEN-TURA IN GROSSETO.

"Signed: PROLETARIAN DEMOCRACY

"What did you understand?"

"That there was a killer in Grosseto."

"Okay, and who is this assassin?"

"Someone who should go to jail."

"Yes, but who is it and what's his name, what did he do?"

" . . . "

"Holy Mother of God, do I have to explain everything to you? Do you even listen when I talk?"

"But, wait, is it . . . is it . . . Fredevventura?"

"Oooh, there we go."

"Sorry, I'd forgotten."

"And now what is he going to do?"

"Come here?"

"Yes. And we, as sincere democratic antifascists must prevent his arrival. Okay?"

I nodded.

We walked alone towards the pier. We didn't have to ask permission from anyone to leave: we were free to move about the harbor, we knew what time to come back. Irma, our dog, was behind us. The blockade of the port lasted for a couple of days, then the shifts on the boats became tiring, medicine, food, human beings expected by sea from one place or another too urgently. The protest was winding down, the ferries were able to dock again, but there were still kids guarding Porto Santo Stefano and keeping an eye on all the passengers to arrive. In turn, the kids on the Direct Action committee stood on the pier performing a sort of customs check on every person who departed. A strip of white cloth on their arms with the hand-written red words "Security Guard" made them recognizable. Suspicious individuals were asked to produce their documents and, in agreement with the mariners working on the ferry, if Ventura were to board the boat would not leave. They called themselves "non collaborators," but a local journal had renamed them "On the Waterfront 2."

Caterina and I went to check on the arrival of the ferries. We were watching everyone who got off, and, if there were suspicious faces, we would elbow each other.

"That lady," Caterina said, "I don't like her: she's too tall, too muscular, she has a faint mustache. I think it's Freda in disguise—let's follow her and see where she goes."

We trailed her to the bakery. She was the baker's sister who lived in Genoa and had come to visit him.

The night of August 30th, at dinner, our mother told us about the first munity attempt in Porto Santo Stefano. There had been eight Carabinieri officials in uniform ready to sail. Before they could set foot on the ferry, the kids who worked at the port convinced the sailors to raise the hatch and release the moorings. At the end of the day, though, the Carabinieri officials were able to make it to their destination. All thanks to the intervention of the priest, who was also waiting to embark on the last ride in full spirit of protest against the delays and for how long they had been held up. He made everyone get on board and ordered the boat to sail. His power to do so had nothing to do with the authority conferred to him by God. Rather, he owned the shipping company and that ferry, the *Rio Marina*, belonged to him and his brother.

That evening, before we fell asleep, Caterina gave me a warning.

"I know that you liked going to the preschool run by the nuns. But luckily this year you'll start school. You can't trust priests and nuns. Did you hear what Mom said? 'Remember: the priest is a traitor.'"

"But what did he do?"

"He is Christian, a Christian Democrat. He's on the side of the Carabinieri and the fascists."

The word "fascist" in my head was a precise synonym for boogeyman.

"But Jesus has nothing to do with this. Jesus is infinitely good."

"Leave Jesus out of it. The Christian Democrats betrayed even him."

"But wasn't that Judas?"

"Forget it, Teresa, go to sleep. Politics isn't your strong suit.

Dream of Jesus, cherubs, and don't make me waste any more time explaining things you don't understand."

"Will you at least tell me a story?"

"Not tonight, I'm tired and tomorrow we have to continue the protest. We need to conserve our energy."

For an entire week we had been underfoot with the Direct Action committee on the docks. We carried around a net and a broomstick handle that we could use as weapons. We kept an eye on the ferries and who got off from afar. Then the news arrived that the mayor of Giglio had surrendered to the dictat from his prefect in Grosseto, who in turn surrendered to the judges of Catanzaro. Freda and Ventura would arrive, along with a procession of eighty Carabinieri officials as an escort. The Direct Action committee responded that the Gigliesi would lock themselves at home in protest, and the visitors would find the island deserted. Caterina and I built a shelter for the occasion. On the hill behind our house there was a large yellow broom plant. We carved a kind of tunnel between the branches, weaving some twigs and cutting others with the help of a pocket knife. It was our hideout. We called it *Rifugio Ginestra*. We brought a cardboard box that we cut in two to make the floor and the door, and some food, snacks, and a towel that served as a pillow or blanket. Fredevventura wouldn't find us there.

Before dawn on Monday, September 6, 1976, while Carabinieri and immovable young men and women faced each other tirelessly between the docks of the port, it was from the sky, on the opposite side of the island, that the men whom everyone was expecting arrived.

Freda and Ventura landed by helicopter on the Campese sports field, evading the distracted Direct Action committee and the distracting, exaggerated surveillance platoon.

Sixteen minutes in a helicopter had been enough to undo days of siege of the port, missed departures, difficult refueling, sleepless nights, and legal charges. Later word would spread that during the flight Freda and Ventura had not exchanged a word. They disembarked at different times, on opposite sides of the helicopter. During their entire stay in Giglio they were never seen together.

Giorgio Freda, alias Franco, was clearly not a sea person. He signalled the importance of his arrival with a fancy suit, like a diva, one who knew he would be watched by many. He wore a blue suit, a well-ironed, light-colored t-shirt in place of his usual turtleneck shirt, and around his neck a white scarf decorated with Hindu motifs, which actually seemed to be holding up his awkwardly large head. White hair, glasses in hand, an extinguished cigar in his mouth. While the gigantic officer on duty helped him take off his life-jacket, he made fun of the fact that he had to bring Tuscan cigars from Puglia because they couldn't be found on the island. Who told him that they couldn't be found here? Tobacco has always been in the sailor's kit. Ventura got off after him. He was more casual in a beige cardigan, short black hair, no beard, the look of an ordinary man. The two of them were loaded in different cars, with an escort of fourteen vehicles, something that had never been seen before on those little streets that were mostly used by Piaggio Apes and donkeys. They were taken to their respective lodgings, but not before the one random un-welcome committee, a group of bricklayers engaged in the construction of a brown house that would forever disfigure the Campese beach, yelled after him, "Have you cowards come to put bombs here too? The granite quarry needs people like you two!"

They didn't pay them any mind, probably because they didn't even hear them over the sound of the helicopter that was leaving and the cross talk of the police officers who surrounded them, constantly touching the holsters of their pistols, even though the most dangerous thing within a half-mile was a jellyfish.

Freda and Ventura found distant accommodations, in two isolated and scenic places. Ventura chose an apartment at the Villaggio Clary, a cluster of small residences not far from the campsite and the Campese beach. His house was nestled in the greenery, hidden among rocks, tufts of bush, and stone steps. He enjoyed an amazing view and sunlight until eight o'clock in the evening. The owner, a Milanese woman with a passion for the sea and a flair for business, had perhaps made a mistake this time, because Ventura's presence scared away the other guests. At eight-thirty in the morning, after setting down his bags, Ventura had already shown up at the lighthouse bar by the harbor to order a cappuccino. It was early and people were still not aware of his airborne arrival. The colonel, however, recognized him. With a firmness that befitted his role, he ordered him to return to his residence, that he couldn't, or rather, that it was not appropriate . . . and thus began Ventura's formal protest: "This is abuse, you'll have to take me away by force." His blatant complaints went on for days: "This town is too expensive, I don't want to pay, the security detail is too oppressive, they listen to my phone calls, they bother me non-stop, prison would be better, where conversations are at least private. They don't let me see my nephews or even my grandmother who is eighty-four years old, I'm like Cesare Pavese, but at least in exile he didn't have all these Carabinieri on him, I should start a hunger strike, I'll put up a tent on the pier." Giovanni Ventura was never quiet; he said everything that crossed his mind—he constantly had to express his thinking, defend his gestures, and let the world know what he was doing.

Freda's exile in Giglio took place at the villa of another Milanese, a former Christian-Democratic consigliere and former lawyer, who took advantage of his retirement to devote himself to the care of a vineyard of white Italian grapes that produced only a few liters of wine each year. The house and the cultivated terraces of the villa were located between two of the most beautiful Giglio beaches, Cannelle and Caldane, on the eastern side of the island. The lawyer's wife had a permit to rent rooms, but Freda was probably staying there for free as a friend. It wasn't hard, seeing him in a bathrobe on the terrace overlooking the sea and hearing the housekeeper answer the telephone, "Mr. Freda isn't available right now," to mistake him for a rich person on vacation. After all, as soon as he got out of the helicopter he assumed that someone would bring him his suitcases.

When Freda arrived with the escort on the narrow slope that leads to the villa from the Cannelle beach, there was only one man walking the shoreline. He was Demos Bonini, a painter from Rimini who fought in the Resistance and after the war founded an advertising agency with Fellini, FeBo. That same evening at dinner with us, Demos had spoken about witnessing the terrorist's arrival and how he had walked all the way up to the gate of the villa.

"All that I saw was a sign that said, 'No trespassing. Three wolf dogs.' It was written just like that, not 'Beware of the dogs,' but 'Three wolf dogs.' To me putting the number there made me laugh. Less funny were the dogs, who were indeed there, and who gave me a good scare, barking like demons. And of course, all three dogs were black. They were fascists too!"

Their laughter didn't reassure me. The monster Fredevventura had made it to Giglio and was at Cannelle, our beach. It took me three more evenings at the grown-ups' table to understand that Freda and Ventura were two different people and to let go of the fantasy in which I'd been completely immersed until that moment.

5.

The day after the arrival of the two terrorists, Red called an
unusual early-afternoon meeting of the Direct Action committee
that went almost deserted. It was as if everyone had suddenly surrendered to the idea that protesting wasn't serving any purpose
and had accepted this without outrage, as one accepts with some
disappointment that it's raining outside. The first deserter was
our father Vittorio. He decided to make use of that beautiful day
with no clouds or wind to take us for a trip on the boat, despite
his wife's indignation. His perspective on the world was indis-
putable to him: "Look at the sun, the sea is flat as glass and
besides, by now, those two have arrived and settled. There's nothing else to do. I'm going out with the girls. Will you come too?"
A question to which he already knew the answer. Elena would
never have gone; she couldn't even imagine how it was possible
to enjoy anything under such circumstances. She simply gave him
a hard look. If that same episode had taken place a few years later
it would have undoubtedly caused a violent fight. As for the
majority of couples, the distinctive features of their respective
characters would provoke an escalating annoyance over time. In
Elena's loving eyes, during their first years together, Vittorio was
someone "who knew how to enjoy life," then he would become
a "superficial" person, before the final verdict of "feckless." For
Vittorio, Elena was at first a "strong-willed" girl, then "one who
takes herself seriously," until the final "pain in the ass."

Meanwhile my sister and I were ready. Caterina would
have certainly gone to the meeting with her mother if it was
not for the prospect of going fishing, an activity at the top of
her preferred pastimes. Irma accompanied us until the boat.
We did everything on auto-pilot: the slippers went in the
cockpit, the padded pillow to lie down on was stored in the
compartment below deck, and we put the bag with the water
bottle and sandwiches in its place. Under the seat on the left

there was the pike pole we always kept on hand. We rigged the oars and kept an eye on the bumpers. We moved fast, sliding a little bit on the blue wooden bottom slippery with saltwater and gasoline. Babbo raised the moorings and from the center of the harbor shouted to the dog to return home. Irma turned her head to the side with a sad look. I was convinced that she was looking right at me and I said to her, "Go!," accompanying my command with a dry gesture that turned into a half salute. I very much would've liked to have brought her, but Dad didn't want to; ever since Irma had stopped hunting with him she had become Irmaporcoddì, a name and epithet together, because nothing she did was useful to him any longer, not even obeying.

We dropped anchor in the bay of Caldane. We were alone. We swam from the boat to the beach. I was cold; before diving in I perched for a long time with my feet gripping the warm edge of the boat and my arms tightly wrapped around my body. Then Babbo called me from the beach. I dove in immediately. My will to please him was always stronger than anything else. Once we were all on the beach, Vittorio pulled out the sandwiches that he had carried through the water in a plastic bag and told us to save some crumbs that we could use later to fish with the corks. After eating I stretched out next to him, digging a small space in the sand by burrowing into it with my back. I worked my way under his arm, leaning my head on his warm, dry skin—Dad's skin was always warm and dry—sneaked a taste of his salty chest, got as close as I could, then closed my eyes and the noises started to blend together, then became more distinct, then blended again, a distant fishing boat, the triple-time cooing of two nearby turtle doves, a newspaper flapping in the wind, the buzzing of a bee emerging from the background of an airplane jet's rumble. Underneath my eyelids the darkness was a mountain veined with violet rivers and a ridge, and little by little I fell asleep.

On the way back we went fishing.

We crumbled the bread into the sea in handfuls and the saddled seabreams appeared in droves. We caught seven of them. Babbo unhooked them and threw them in the bucket, without water: they had gutted mouths, hooks entering through their palates and exiting out their eyes. I tried to avoid looking at them; I could hear the sound of their tails flapping, I could feel them wiggling in their own blood and shit. Babbo told me many times that fish cannot feel pain, trying to explain something to me about their cerebral cortex. I trusted him, he was a veterinarian. But if they didn't suffer, why were they so agitated? And who had ever been in their skin and could say so for sure? When the boat stopped in the harbor, the sound of the fish slapping against the plastic came less often. I took the bucket. I looked at the chrome and red tangle of the fish in agony. I knew that if I had thrown them all into the sea at that moment it would have been in time, they would have started swimming again, crookedly and slowly at first, but eventually they would have disappeared into the deep, alive even with a broken mouth. I lifted the bucket and I put it on the side of the boat: a small movement to make it fall would have been enough to set them all free. But at that moment Babbo looked at me and winked from under his thick dark eyebrows. I couldn't betray him. I put the bucket back where it had been and didn't look at it again until they finished banging around. Back home Caterina ran to Mom with the bucket to show her the loot. Mom was very angry; she was on the sofa reading, bent over herself, and said, "Yes, beautiful, but take them away, they stink, I don't want to see them." Caterina replied to her, "You really are obnoxious—tonight I won't let you taste even a bite." She replied, "What a shame, without your bloody fish I'll starve to death." They were like that: they fought like two little girls, my sister treated her as an equal. Vittorio had the audacity to ask her how the meeting had gone. Without even raising her eyes from under the book she responded, "Poorly, thanks! There were five of us, and still people wonder why this country is going to shit. Tonight I don't want you in my way. I tried to call another meeting, but you don't need to participate, you don't care about anything anymore, do you?"

Babbo didn't even answer her. To us he said, "Okay girls, now we'll go to Castello and tomorrow, if it is nice, we'll go to the lighthouse." Mom's voice came from the other room: "But tomorrow won't be nice." I was cutting out a paper-doll dress and I wanted to throw the scissors at her.

Babbo said, "Let's go." He made us put on more layers and without even taking a shower we went out. Caterina brought the plastic bag of fish with her. Irma followed us. We found Sergio, who was going to Castello, to Biagio's house. He said that we could come too, since there were so many of us. We climbed into his bright green Dyane. Babbo tried to convince Irma to get in the trunk. "Go!" he ordered her. Irma didn't move. "Get in, I said!" Irma sat there, and watched him with big eyes, terrorized, motionless. "Irmaporcoddì!" He grabbed her by the scruff and lifted her up, throwing her into the back. From the back seat, I leaned over to caress her. My father said to me in a strange voice, "I didn't hurt her, don't worry, it's just that she doesn't obey—she can't always do whatever the fuck she wants!" I stayed quiet and so did Caterina. "These fish are so smelly," said Sergio turning his neck, "why don't we throw them out the car window? Corinna's behind us, it would be hilarious if it rained mullets on her hood."

"These aren't mullets," said Caterina, holding on more tightly to the bag full of her catch.

At Castello, Biagio served pasta with clams, a frittata, and salads, and his wife put the fish in the freezer: she said they would grill them another time, it wasn't the right time to set up the grill and all. Caterina was furious—she kept saying, but we brought fresh fish, let's eat them, I don't want frittata, I want the seabream, Babbo, they'll end up eating them later but they're ours, we caught them ourselves. My father told her to shut up, that we would come and eat them here another time; he hated my sister's impertinent sincerity in public because it shattered his good-mannered persona, his desire, almost a necessity, to always make a good impression.

After dinner, we went to the cellar, where Biagio kept the wine barrels. Another dozen people arrived to drink and smoke. There were also some German tourists. Caterina and I sat on a bench in a corner, careful not to touch the wall of moldy rock with our backs. We were silent as we peeled the cigarette burns from the plastic tablecloth to make the stuffing come out, among the unerasable circles of red wine. I would suck a tuft of still salty hair, Caterina would intermittently ask to leave, Babbo would say we'd go soon. Then he gave us two plastic glasses into which he poured a little orange juice from a bottle he found on a dusty shelf. He told us that he had to leave for ten minutes because he had to drive home a woman who was staying in Campese and didn't know how to get back there at that time of night. Caterina said we'd come too. He replied, "No, don't worry, I'll just be ten minutes, wait here for me, then when I get back we can go home."

The woman, a lanky blonde with very pale skin, waved to us from the door. Caterina didn't wave back. Instead she began to spit in the glass of orange juice, very seriously. I imitated her. Then we put the glasses that we had spit in on the other side of the table and began cackling at the idea that sooner or later one of the drunkards would drink from one of them. They were smoking. No one was watching us.

Our game of spitting in the glasses eventually stopped being fun. Dad wasn't coming back. Caterina decided to leave the moldy cellar and walk around Castello. It was humid, kind of foggy. The paths of Castello were a confusing labyrinth to me. I didn't want to go further away, I knew that I wouldn't be able to get back to the cellar, but Caterina took my hand. "Come, I am going to show you something. But promise that you won't get scared." We passed through two empty alleys and the steps that led to Scipione's café. Caterina was dragging me. Every time, when we were in the darkest corners, she would howl to make me more scared. I would yell. We got to the front of the church. The courtyard was lit up by the moon. She told me that we had to go inside.

"But we can't."

"Yes we can, the Lord's house is always open."

"Okay, then give me your hand."

She pushed open the big door with her shoulder; it was cold and dark. I don't know why the church was unlocked. Maybe in Giglio they never locked it.

"I'm going to show you something."

We skirted alongside the wall until we came to a lit alcove. Inside was a relic, the remains of San Mamiliano, his arm preserved in a kind of silver case.

"Here lie the bones of the deeeeaad!" howled Caterina before letting go of my hand and starting to run toward the door. I couldn't lose her: I chased her, yelling her name, while she, running faster and faster, yelled at me to watch out, that there were ghosts in the well in the piazza. The ghosts of fascists and traitorous priests.

Why did she amuse herself by scaring me like that? Why did I always fall for it? Predictably, I tripped up on a slab of granite, scraped my knees, and without getting back up started crying and insulting her. She turned back toward me. She helped me up and told me that it wasn't a big deal even though I had torn my shorts and my knees were bleeding. She took my hand again. I couldn't stop crying. We went back to the cellar but Dad hadn't come back yet. We waited outside for him.

Vittorio returned revitalized, but he didn't realize how badly I was hurt.

Caterina attacked him: "How long was that? You know that it's extremely late? Look, Teresa is hurt. You didn't even notice that she's crying. This fool tore up her shorts while running in the churchyard."

"It's your fault, you imbecile!" I yelled at her.

Vittorio told us not to argue, that we would go home. He didn't lose his smile.

He went into the cellar to tell Sergio that we had to return to the port. By the time we left it was almost one in the morning. Sergio was stumbling, losing and reestablishing his balance after every step with a rhythm so steady that he seemed to be memorizing a choreography. At that hour, Castello was completely surrounded by fog, and I was terrified of returning home in his car. Caterina was insisting to Dad: "Tell him you should drive, I'm begging you."

How many times have we risked our lives coming down from Castello in a car with someone who has drunk too much? How many times have we weaved between those unlit sharp bends, with cliffs to mark the edge of the road? Every time I imagine the scene: the car that didn't swerve in time and flew down, flipping and crashing to the water. Back then on Giglio there were the remnants of two cars. One was totally rusted, the original white visible between the curves of the Campese. The other one, which had caught fire, had almost made it to the water, on the slope toward the Cannelle beach. They remained there to make the view between the myrtle and strawflower bushes more frightening with their aura of death.

Dad told Caterina to not worry, that Sergio was always careful behind the wheel, even more so when he'd been drinking: he'd never been in an accident. And I, as usual, believed it, but I held my sister's hand tightly and I prayed the prayers that the nuns had taught me. In those days children were not so central. They were the side dish. There were alcoholics behind the wheel and parents who trusted them. And, naturally, the god of the drunks protected them.

At the top of the Arenella, Sergio swiped the side mirror of a parked car in front of the gas station. He cursed. He didn't slow down, and no one spoke until we were outside the house. With the engine off, before getting out, a horrendous, dank smell overtook the car's cabin: Irma had vomited in the trunk.

6.

The day before I started school, Cate and I had gone down to the beach to pretend to be gymnasts. That summer Nadia Comăneci had excelled at the Olympics and we had spent whole afternoons imitating her, trying to somersault, to cartwheel, falling on our backs with our necks bent and getting covered in sand. We were always champions. We would take turns as gymnast and judge, and if we were really bad we gave each other 9/10, otherwise it was 10/10 or 10/10 with distinction.

Even Irma came. We pretended that she was one of our challengers, the American competitor that always lost, and every time she jumped after us we would give her a 4/10. We told her that she was a terrible gymnast and then started laughing.

Usually we took up half the beach.

During a triple cartwheel with a corkscrew jump, I almost hit the wall of the bar. On my last frenzied leap, I kicked up a plume of sand that landed on a man who was leaning against the light granite wall to read.

"Jesus! Look what you did!" he yelled at me, shaking the sand from his pages with one hand and wiping his face with the other.

I got up from the sand, my head spinning. I said timidly, "Excuse me . . ."

"Eh, excuse me my ass," he said closing his book, "try to be more careful! With all the space you have, do you really need to play right next to me?"

I blushed. If there's a thing that I've never learned, it's how to accept criticism. I've never been able to react well to it.

Caterina and Irma got closer. "Sir, if my sister had seen you, she would definitely have been more careful, but you aren't visible from that corner over there, especially on this side because we had the sun in our eyes, and your jacket blends in with the granite. So please forgive her, she didn't do it on purpose."

He replied, "It's always someone's fault if something happens. Nothing happens by itself or by chance. If you had been paying more attention, you wouldn't have hit me."

With that remark, my sister planted her feet in the sand, pushed her auburn bangs off her forehead, rested her hand like a canopy over her eyes to protect herself from the sun, and looked him in the eyes. With her other hand she took Irma by the collar and held her tight like you do with fierce dogs, even though Irma sat up with the most harmless look on her face, her tongue hanging out. I stayed on the sidelines and understood that my sister was about to open her mouth again and there would be trouble.

"Mister, what did you say? Did I misunderstand or did you really say that it's always someone's fault if something happens? Look, I know who you are." She paused to catch her breath. "My sister is guilty of having thrown sand on you, and she even apologized to you. We'll be leaving now. But you . . . have you ever apologized to anyone for what you did? Huh? You should apologize too! Apologize for all the deaths at Piazza Fontana. Apologize to all of Italy. Ask for forgiveness and then we'll be even. Actually, no, we won't be even at all until you're in prison. You'll see, you'll be fine in there. No one will throw sand at you in jail." Then she threw another handful of sand at him and shouted, "Down with the fascists, long live liberty," ending her political diatribe with a gesture of childish arrogance.

Astounded, the white-haired man remained motionless for a few seconds. Then he stood up. "What the hell are you going on about? What're you saying? How dare you?" He looked around quickly, saw that no one was around, and slapped Caterina. It was a slap that turned her head. The man turned and walked toward the villas without saying anything. We responded to that unexpected event in an unforeseeable way: Caterina remained silent and didn't even shed a single tear. Irma began to bark, even if she wasn't able to because she never did. Her throat was choked by some hoarse howls, like the moans of a seagull. I, meanwhile, began to insult that man as he walked away. I shouted all the curse words I knew louder and louder: "Worm! Fucking coward! You filthy, piss-drinking, horny, slobbering prick! I'm going to tell my dad and then you'll see! You make me sick and your jacket is the color of shit! Fuck you, you stupid fucking pussy!" The veins of my neck bulged and my face blushed red. Caterina put her hand over my mouth and said, "Stop it, you idiot! Do you want him to kill us? Don't you know who that is?"

"No, it can't be."

"Yes," Caterina answered, "it's really him."

"Well, now he's gone home to get his gun and then he'll come to get us. You're so stupid, Cate."

"Let's get out of here," she urged me, starting to run like crazy, with Irma behind her. Terrified, I tried to chase them. But I had on wooden clogs and, as usual, I fell on the first yard of asphalt after the beach, reopening the scabs on my knees. I got back up right away and kept on running with my clogs in hand, trying to keep low to dodge any bullets that might come from the villa.

But no bullet came. At home, I disinfected my wounds by pouring hydrogen peroxide over them, making them sizzle and foam. We spent the rest of the afternoon in the *Rifugio Ginestra* to devise plans to escape the terrorist's vendetta. At dinner, without even planning to, we didn't say anything about what had happened.

That evening, we had to get ready for the first day of school. We distracted ourselves by arranging our clothes on the edge of our chairs for the next day: a clean T-shirt, cotton socks, the blue smock that everyone wore, boys and girls alike. I checked the contents of my schoolbag a thousand times, lined up some freshly sharpened pencils of various lengths in my hand-me-down pencil case, stuffed in my ruler and eraser under the rubber bands and sniffed them hard before closing it. I thought that I'd never be able to fall asleep. But soon enough I drifted off. I dreamed that my teacher was a white-haired man who looked down at me.

I ended up in Caterina's bed, like I always did when I got scared, but said nothing to her. For the next few weeks we avoided going to the sea by ourselves. We stayed at home, we pretended to do lots of homework, we spent a lot of time at the *Rifugio* or at the hotel with Mom and Dad, who were pleasantly surprised by our sudden attachment to them. But I kept having nightmares. I started peeing the bed again, and because I was ashamed, I tried to not drink in the evenings. I secretly put a towel on the mattress and if it happened, I would silently run to the bathroom to change and put all the wet stuff in the dirty laundry basket. Nonnalina obviously noticed and told Elena, who one evening decided to investigate when she kissed me goodnight.

"So, Teresa, do you like going to school?"

"Yep."

"Do you have fun with your classmates or is there someone who teases you?"

"I'm having fun. My friends are the same. I was sitting at the same table as Pietro, but they separated us because we talk too much."

"And your teacher, how is he?"

"He's good."

"So everything is going alright?"

"Yup."

"And you're not afraid of anything?"

"No."

"So why are you peeing yourself at night and having night-mares?"

". . ."

"Don't worry, Teresa, these things happen and there's nothing to worry about. I just wanted to know if there's anything in particular that's bothering you."

". . ."

"Look, you can tell me anything. You don't need to be embarassed about anything with your mom. What do you dream about that scares you so much?"

"That Fredevventura will chase after me and Caterina and kill us. I'm wearing my clogs and I fall and I get left behind. Caterina runs up to a cliff, but I can't climb so I grab onto a daisy that breaks off and he gets closer and closer . . ."

"How silly you are! And why didn't you say something right away? Look, there's really no danger. They can't hurt any-one now. Did you see that the Carabinieri always keep them under control? Why are you afraid?"

"Caterina told me that if he finds us, he'll kill us."

"But who's going to kill you two?"

I fessed up confusedly, sobbing.

"Fredevventura, at the Cannelle beach. I mean, I don't know, either Freda or Ventura, I don't know which one. It was a man. I threw sand at him but I didn't do it on purpose and he got angry so Caterina told him off and then we ran away."

The police chief summoned Caterina, who was questioned by herself. The defendant tried to play it down, blaming my imagination as a small child. She said we saw a guy on the beach who looked like Freda and, by mistake, while we were playing, some sand had ended up on him, but he moved and it all ended there. Mom didn't believe her, or rather, blamed her for encouraging my imagination. Caterina withstood the accusations and swallowed the scolding, but when we were alone she twisted my ear while gritting her teeth in anger: "What got into your head to make you tell her? Idiot!"

I said that Mom had asked me what I was dreaming about and I told her about my nightmare, but I didn't tell her the story about the slap and all that. It was immediately clear between us sisters that we shouldn't talk about how Caterina got slapped, not then, not ever. I don't think I realized that telling the whole story would have amplified the impact of the event. I only knew that Caterina wanted it that way. I knew it and that was enough for me to obey her. She had defended me again and I hadn't been able to defend her. And, for her, obedience was the only way I could show my gratitude.

Caterina, the sun, me in her shadow.

Caterina crying in anger, me laughing for no reason.

Caterina with her stories, me, her audience.

Caterina, the lawyer, me, the acquitted client.

Caterina the red-head, among the brambles and dry grass, me dark-skinned, among the poppies and broom shrubs.

Caterina, the mainland, me, the lesser island.

7.

For the next few days Caterina avoided me. We would leave for school together and we would always come back together, escorted by Irma, but during the long afternoons which we were gifted by the warm end of that September, Caterina isolated herself with her drawings, her homework, and reading the newspapers. During my after-school snack, which I ate silently behind her hunched shoulders as she moved her hand very quickly to outline a dark background, I got tired.

One day when I got out of school I asked Pietro if I could go over to his house to do homework. He told me that he didn't do his homework and I, despite my disapproval of his choice, suggested that we play together that afternoon. He gave me a time, 3:00 P.M., to meet on the stairs below my house. He wanted to show me something but he couldn't show it to me in the house.

I was excited. I finished my homework quickly and then waited in the courtyard well before our scheduled time. I played with Irma; I threw her a piece of stiff, blue, knotted old rope and she brought it back to me a bit reluctantly, covered in drool. Pietro arrived after 4:00 P.M. He said to me, "Come on! It's almost too late to go to the spot." He held a plastic bag with something inside. Based on the smell, I imagined it was live bait. I followed him with Irma. When Pietro saw that my dog was following us, he protested: "She can't come. She'll bother us. Put her back in the courtyard and tie her up." I quickly put her behind the gate and closed it against her while she dug with her feet and stuck her nose through the bars.

Pietro started walking at a fast clip toward the green lighthouse, then he turned left before the fountain of San Giorgio and walked along a narrow street that went between houses and continued toward the country road, following the path of a pipe that at a certain point went into the bushes and seemed to go nowhere. The path wound past a huge block of granite, the base of the mountain on which the port was built. We jumped up on the rocks and kept climbing toward the top among dry broom shrubs, strawflowers, and prickly pears until the cliff became so steep that we were forced to crawl on all fours. I was curious to know where he wanted to take me. I was afraid of getting hurt or that we would go too far, but I didn't say anything, I just followed him and imitated his nimble steps. We got to a really high point where the grey rock was broken into slanted steps, like a series of petrified waves. Past the second step, Pietro told me to slow down and move quietly. We got flat on the rock and proceeded with caution, holding our breaths, our hearts pounding. Having made it under the third rock spike, Pietro told me to stay still with my head down while he pulled himself up just enough to peek over the ledge. He turned to me with a very excited look and said, "They're here still, but go slowly, don't let them see you." He gestured for me to look out. I pulled myself up slowly. A couple of meters ahead was a big nest of herring gulls, with two newborns who were standing on a messy heap of grass. They had grey feathers, their beaks were only a bit darker, and they cried out awkwardly for food. They weren't very cute.

Pietro pulled me down and we began to whisper.

"Let's be careful," he said, "if the mother bird sees us, it's capable of gouging out our eyes. We don't know if these two will survive. They were born a few days ago; tomorrow someone might eat them."

"Someone who? Nobody eats seagulls."

"No, huh? When they're so little they can be eaten by hawks, crows, cats, even other seagulls."

"But what are you saying? Seagulls don't eat other seagulls. Come on!"

He wanted to raise his voice to argue his point, but he couldn't. He turned red in the face trying to control his anger.

"Now watch what happens!" He opened the small plastic bag that he had been carrying the whole time, tied to the loops of his ripped jeans. It was full of leftover fish, octopus tentacles, anchovy batter, and bread. He began throwing handfuls of it around the nest. The mother bird arrived first, a white and grey seagull with a huge wingspan. She landed and looked around. She looked at us but didn't seem to really see us, at least not as a threat to her nest. She was more interested in the food. She ate two pieces of octopus and began giving the rest to her young. Then another big seagull arrived, probably the father bird, because they took turns feeding their young. Dad had explained to me that seagulls make families, and both the male and female brood and feed their young before they leave them. Within a minute, three other adult herring gulls came. While trying to steal the baby bird's prey, they injured his eye. And at that point they began to pile on him, while the mother bird released a scream, waving her big wings, and turning her head in bursts, with her fixed yellow eye, stupid and cruel. Pietro jumped up from our shelter, clapping his hands to shoo them all away, yelling, "Did you see it? Did you see how they do kill each other?" The two baby birds were still in the nest, one alive and the other mortally wounded. Pietro took the wounded bird and snapped its neck. *Snap*, it popped. "This way he won't suffer. A bird can't live blind. Anyway, the parents will return soon, you'll see." He took the dead chick from the nest and threw it far.

Pietro and I started to run away.

While I was running I insulted him. "Are you stupid Pietro? Look what happened! You're such an asshole, you're a murderer! And anyway, it didn't eat the baby bird, I was the one who was right!"

"Oh, but it wasn't me, eh! It was you who didn't believe that they killed each other! I only gave them something to eat!"

I ran fast down the cliff, leaving it behind me. I kept yelling insults at him. He replied, "Look, I didn't want to do it. What did I know?"

When we made it to the fountain, we stopped to catch our breath and drink.

He told me, "I only wanted to bring them something to eat and show you the nest. Did you like the nest at least?"

"It was nice, but I prefer seagulls alive."

"I didn't want it to suffer! It was already blinded. Anyway, seagulls are cruel animals."

"They're animals, they aren't good or bad. You, on the other hand, are bad. Because you did it on purpose."

I started running home again. Pietro yelled my name once, then he let me go. I went to the *Rifugio Ginestra*. I was scared.

I heard the *snap* in my ears. I thought back to the bloody eye of the little seagull. And then, *snap*. In some oblique way, I had realized that people liked to scare me. They took satisfaction in proving to me an evil that I didn't believe in, and I didn't understand why.

The next day we acted like nothing happened. But I was afraid of Pietro.

When the bell rang he came out after me and stopped me. "I brought you something."

He handed me a big box of matches. It was blue and on top there was the figure of a lady wearing a long skirt in a cloud of white smoke.

I liked it.

"What is it?"

"A gift. Because you like animals."

I didn't say anything. I slid the drawer open gently. Inside was a shiny black beetle. Pietro had painted a T in red paint on its shell.

"A bug."

"Yes, but this one is unique. Did you see what I did to it?"

"Yeah. T for Teresa. Thanks."

"Now you have to keep it in a safe spot. Give it a name and something to eat and he is yours." I closed the box and put it in the pocket of my smock. My sister, who left a bit late, caught up with me for the walk home. I didn't say anything to her and we walked almost the whole way in silence.

After lunch I snuck away to my room to grab my box, and left on my own. I went to the *Rifugio Ginestra* and freed the bug when I got there. It climbed carefully up and out over the side of the box. I put him on my hand and resisted the tickle and the grossness of his thin black feet.

I heard Caterina come in from behind.

"What are you playing with?"

"With a bug."

"Let me see."

I showed it to her.

"Did you do that red T?"

"No. Pietro gave it to me as a gift."

"You brought Pietro to this *Rifugio*? I knew you were a traitor!"

"Nooo. He gave it to me at school."

"And yesterday what did you do with Pietro? I saw you with him."

"He discovered a seagull nest with two hatchlings and we went to see them."

"You have to be careful—seagulls are mean, especially if they have hatchlings."

"I know already, okay?"

"By the way. Do you know what beetles eat?"

"No, I tried to give it some grass but it didn't want it."

She laughed. "I believe that it didn't want it."

"Why, because it's *carnivolous*?"

She laughed even louder.

"If anything it's carnivorous! No, not even. You know what beetles like?"

"..."

"Shit! It eats dung, which, in a word that you can understand, is poop."

I couldn't understand how serious she was.

I smiled, making a disgusted face.

"There you go. Your friend Pietro gave you a beautiful gift. You can see that he really cares about you. He gave you a trinket with your initial. A beautiful trinket of shit."

She took the beetle, left the *Rifugio*, and threw it far, into the middle of a bush.

"It was gross but it was mine. You could've asked me before throwing it away."

"No strangers or dung beetles are allowed in this shelter, bird brain! And if you bring Pietro here, we're no longer sisters."

"I won't bring him here. But the beetle was a gift for me. Now go find it."

She got up to leave the den.

"I'm going to read the newspaper. You go look for your dung ball if you care about it so much."

8.

In Nonnalina's room there was a wooden picture frame with five ovals. In each oval there was a black and white photograph of a man. They were all young men, except one who was older and had a mustache. They were all pale and unsmiling. They looked alike even though one of them looked like a little girl. The one with the saddest eyes was the grandfather that we had never met.

The lives of those men were a secret. We couldn't talk about them. Nonnalina rarely spoke in general, and when she did it was in dialect and never about her past. One day, while I was sitting on her bed, she insisted on tying my shoes even though I knew how to do it myself (she always did it too tight: she would pull tight the laces as if they'd never have to be untied, as if I had to walk across the land for hours), and I asked her:

"Nonna, were those men next to Grandpa his brothers?"

"Yes."

"And that one with the mustache, was he their dad?"

"Uh-huh."

"And they are all dead?"

"Yes."

"But why?"

She pulled the laces a bit tighter and tied the knot.

"Did they die in the war?" I pressed.

"The war had already ended."

"Then how'd it happen?"

"Let's go. And enough with all these questions," she said.

She said it with thin, bleached lips that tightened into a grimace which I had never seen before. I didn't ask any more questions. And I got down, like she had asked me to.

It would take me some more time to learn what had happened, and it wasn't directly from my grandmother, but rather, like almost everything else, through the dirty filter of my sister's words.

It was at the end of her fifth and my first year of elementary school. Caterina had to do an assignment on oral history. The class had to conduct an interview to present as their project for the end-of-year exam: "I Heard Talk of the War . . . an interview with an elderly person who lived through it."

What Caterina wrote took up half a lined notebook, which was used only for the interview. The assignment earned her her usual 10/10 with distinction, a phone call to our mother to learn how much of it was true, the concern of her teacher, and, above all, an absolute ban on reading to the other children what she'd written.

But that rule applied only in school. And the secrecy of the forbidden notebook was short-lived between us. School had already ended the afternoon that she read it to me, and I had just turned seven years old. Our mother was working at full speed, meanwhile Vittorio was rarely at the hotel. He would fish a bit, walk around with the excuse of accompanying the customers visiting the island, and he would only appear when he wanted to, and escape as soon as he saw Red's complaints gathering on the horizon.

Cate and I were almost always on our own. Every so often some girls would come over to play with us but that was a rare occurrence, which would end with me entertaining our guests while Caterina left to do something else when she got bored. She didn't like the company of children, and she didn't like their games. During the winter, the refuge we'd built among the broom shrubs had been destroyed by the wind and the rain. In the spring, a tangle of branches hung over the entrance and it would've been too difficult to clear it. We would've needed an adult, and, at that point, it wouldn't be a secret anymore. Instead, we sat in the garden, went to the beach with Nonnalina, or hung out on the rocks in front of the hotel.

That afternoon, however, Caterina took me somewhere else. I think she did it on purpose, to avoid contaminating a place we visited often with her story. Because she knew that it would traumatize me. About a third of a mile from home, at the place where the homes on the port ended, there were vegetable gardens. They had been built on terraces with little land, near a ridge of rocks which a thin stream of water flowed through, when it wasn't dry. Above the gardens was a fence where Dad kept two of his dogs, the hunting dogs, a pointer and an Italian spinone, feisty and smelly, always ready to run away. We didn't consider them ours at all because, for us, Irma was the only dog. Above the doghouse we also had another small enclosure with two chickens. Usually Nonnalina would bring leftovers to the dogs and gather eggs. It was her only daily walk besides the one she made to the store to buy groceries. After lunch Caterina asked Nonna if that day we could go instead. Nonna said yes, so long as we were careful about the cars and not letting the dogs escape when we opened the gate, and that we also gave them some water, that we brought dry bread to the chickens, that we didn't scare them, that we didn't break the eggs, and an entire list of exhortations that ended with *come straight home when you've finished.*

We took care of the chores in two minutes. At that point, Caterina sat down on the overturned red wheelbarrow and picked up her little backpack.

"So you want to know what happened to Grandpa?"

"Grandpa who?"

"Grandpa on Nonnalina's side, Mom's dad."

"Do you know what happened to his brothers, too?"

"Yeah."

" . . ."

"Are you sure you want to know now? Look, it's an awful thing. You'll never forget it."

"Yes. I want to know. But who told *you*?"

"Nonna herself."

"Nonna never talks about Grandpa."

"She told *me* everything. I wrote it down in here," she said, throwing open her notebook. "Now I'll read it to you."

She made me swear not to cry and to not talk about it with anyone, not even Mom. I swore, without knowing how much it would cost me. She cleared her throat. She paused.

"The title is this, I Heard Talk of the War . . . an interview with an elderly person who lived through it."

She took a breath.

"I interviewed my nonna, who lived through the war when she was young. At first, she told me she didn't remember anything, and I had to press her. My nonna comes from Romagna and spoke in dialect the whole time. I've transcribed her answers in formal Italian so you'll understand better.

"Nonna, how old were you when the war started?

"Twenty-one or twenty-two. When your grandpa was dis-

charged, we got married. It was 1943. And we were already displaced. Your mom was born while we were displaced.

"What does displaced mean?

"That they'd bombed our home and we had to flee. We stayed in a farmhouse with three families. We lived in the stables, and when your mother was born I had a hemorrhage, but they wouldn't let me lay on the bed because otherwise I would ruin the mattress, and we only had the one. They made me a straw bed and the midwife put some newspaper under me to soak up the bleeding. Your mom was born with the news printed on her back.

"And what did it say?

"That the Americans had bombed Bologna. The war was about to end.

"And when it ended, what did you all do? Did you celebrate?

"When the war ended, your mom and I moved to your grandpa's house, with my sister-in-law and her daughter. It was just the girls and women.

"And where were the men?

"The men were hiding because they didn't want to fight anymore. The fascists wanted to draft them again to fight for them, but they didn't want to. They wanted to wait for everything to end so they could go back to working the land.

"And then what happened?

"They hid so that not even we knew where they were. Near our house there was a German commando unit. One day, the Germans left. They set everything on fire and left. The next day, Grandpa, his two brothers, and their father returned home.

"The war was over, the Germans had gone away, and the men of the family had come back home. So you celebrated!

"Yes. Our liberation lasted a day. Only a day. We had tagliatelle with goose ragù on the table outside under the mulberry trees. It was September. My brother-in-law Dino said, "Finally we are free," and his father replied, "I don't know if we're free." He wasn't sure if everything was over. And he was right.

"*The next day a group of blackshirts arrived at our house with trucks and rifles.*

"*Who were the blackshirts?*

"*Fascists.*

"*But were they Italian or German?*

"*Italian. They were from our area, they spoke our dialect.*

"*What happened?*

"*They kicked us women and girls out of the house and kept the men inside. Shots and screams rang out. They tortured them. The youngest, Silvio, had his hands nailed to the table. My sister-in-law ran away looking for help and never returned. I stayed on my own with the two little girls near the well. The two of them cried and I couldn't calm them down. Then, after an hour, they brought the men out. They were all bloody. I tried to approach my husband but he told me to go away. One of them knocked me aside with his gun. We spoke to each other with our eyes. They took them all to the bank of the Santerno River and shot them. But your grandpa wasn't killed because he jumped down into the riverbed before they shot him. That was the war.*

"*But why did they kill them, Nonna? What had they done?*

"*Nothing. They'd done nothing.*"

Caterina closed the notebook and looked right at me.

"I know that you don't believe it, but she really told me all this. Before writing it up, I asked Mom if she would proofread it. She said it was all true. She even told me that she remembered seeing her dad all bloody and her mom rub her face in the dirt. But that can't be true because she was only a year old when it happened. Small children can't retain memories."

I stood up. Obviously, there were many things that I hadn't understood. But I didn't want explanations. I would've liked to take that notebook and throw it to the dogs, to destroy everything that was written there, to make myself forget about it. I was angry with myself. Why had I said yes once again to Caterina?

My sister looked satisfied.

We didn't speak on the way home. Caterina took me by the hand. The wind had picked up. In the garden, our nonna was sweeping the pine needles. I couldn't look at her. I took out the egg that I'd gotten from the hen house and was about to give it to her, but I dropped it. Nonna cursed. She started to bend down to clean it but I stopped her. I squeezed her hard under her bosom, where I could reach, and started bawling into her apron, which smelled like onions and detergent. "I didn't mean it, I'm sorry, I'm sorry, I'm sorry," I repeated.

"What's the big deal? Calm down!"

And when she saw that I didn't stop crying, she pulled me away from her.

"It's nothing," she said. "Nothing." In Italian.

INTERLUDE
(1979)

9.

Despite my nightmares full of flightless birds with savage beaks being tormented by an older sister, and basically ignored by my parents, my childhood was happy.

I wasn't an orphan, I wasn't poor, I had never experienced war, or suffered from hunger. I wasn't ugly, or sick, or the victim of violence, or, despite what my sister had tried to make me believe, stupid. But I knew that in other times and in other places there had been war, hunger, ugliness, ignorance, wickedness, and casualties. There were towns that were always cold and cities full of concrete and cars. I had an island, and the fortune of spending the majority of my time with the sea as my horizon. I was surrounded by a liquid seat belt that always protected me from everything that happened *out there*. Almost always.

There was an evening, toward the end of February in 1979, when the hotel was closed. We had dinner with just us women. Vittorio had left with a group of friends on a hunting trip to Croatia, somewhere all the game hadn't been killed off yet.

"Teresa's slice is bigger," complained Caterina, looking at the tart on her plate. "As usual."

Nonna said that that wasn't true and that I had to get bigger anyway, because I was thin.

"You see? You can't even deny it. You've admitted that hers is bigger and that she needs to grow, poor thing, the undernourished girl. And, as always, I get the smaller piece. In this family, fairness just doesn't exist."

Mom took the serving dish with the leftover tart and replaced Caterina's plate with it.

"Here, eat all of it if you want. It's yours, you mistreated little girl. Eat it! In this family without justice or liberty, not only can you have the bigger slice, you can even have the whole tart. Do you feel bad, are you getting fat? In this family, there's room for everyone."

"I never said that I wanted all of it for myself, Mom."

"You said that you always get the smaller pieces. There you go, have the biggest bit."

"You always exaggerate everything. I didn't say that. I said that Nonna never cuts equal-sized pieces. But maybe it's normal given that she lived in a world where justice and equality didn't exist: there was the boss, the sharecropper, the farmhand, there were men who got the best parts, and the women had to be happy with the rest. If you grow up among injustice, it is difficult to perform justice afterward . . ."

Nonna, who had already begun washing the plates, told her to stop without averting her eyes from the sink. But Red didn't let it go.

"Don't you dare, Caterina, ever offend your grandmother with such insults. You're just an arrogant know-it-all who's stupidly jealous of your sister. What do you know about your grandma's life?"

"I know a lot more than you think. And anyway, I'm not stupidly jealous, I'm objective. You treat her better," she said, pointing at me with her fork.

"Has the thought never occurred to you that we treat *her* better because she treats *us* better? Because your favorite sport is offending other people?"

"See! You admit that you treat her better."

Watching them argue up close stunned me. It was like

seeing someone rant at themselves in a warped mirror. Caterina had filled out and had grown her hair. She was a scaled-down copy of our mother.

"Stop it!" Nonna continued begging them to stop, without success.

They would have gone on for hours to have the last word. I intervened: "Come on, Mom, Cate didn't mean to offend anybody."

"That's right, I just wanted an explanation for a repeated injustice, and I was hoping that it wasn't the result of unequal treatment. But clearly, as everyone tells me, it is!"

"You're exaggerating, Caterina! Now go to your room!"

"Great, we've come to orders and punishments. Yes, ma'am," said Caterina imitating a military salute.

With her soapy rubber gloves, Nonna turned the TV volume up to drown them out. There was a newscast. With a wave of her hand my mom descended into silence. Nonna turned off the faucet and we all listened.

"You're connected to the Assize Court of Catanzaro. President Scuteri is about to read the sentence for the bombing of Piazza Fontana." The camera panned to the jury and then to the president of the court, who began, "In the name of the Italian people, the Assize Court of Catanzaro, pursuant to articles 483, 488 and 489 of the criminal procedural code, declares Freda, Franco; Ventura, Giovanni; and Giannettini Guido guilty of the felony of terrorism and sentences them to life imprisonment."

My sister started running around the kitchen, shoving her left hand repeatedly into the crook of her right elbow, saying, "Take that, take that, take that, you rotten bastard!"

I laughed.

"Caterina," Mom said, "Calm down! They won't serve a day in jail. Freda has been in Costa Rica for a while already and they broke Ventura out a month ago and no one can find him. By now he'll be on some Mexican beach."

Archival images followed: we saw the funerals for the victims in Piazza Duomo in Milan, a square packed with people, a square in black and white but especially grey, thousands of people and many politicians—Andreotti, Rumor, Tanassi. In another shot we saw Freda's white head and Ventura's beard, a people's protest and a march with a familiar-looking banner and a small crowd gathered in front of the sea. And then, for at least two never-ending seconds, two immeasurable fragments of time, the TV broadcast a close-up of my mother's hair, her eyes shining with severity and anger. I shouted, "Mom! It's you!" Then the image turned back to the court again. More interviews followed, other people and many words, but I wasn't listening to them. I'd just seen my mom on TV. I saw her face in the black rectangle that was a window into the world, the real one that existed beyond, and the fake world too, made up of cartoons and everything else that happened but wasn't part of our life on the island which seemed so distant from everything, but my mother was there inside it and simultaneously a foot away from me, and all of a sudden everything got closer and became ours, and that moment was the epiphany of my childhood that enshrined her once and for all as a supernatural being, my mother-of-pearl, the one who knew and made history, the woman—like my grandmother, for that matter—whom I could never live up to. And our isolated world, now that it had appeared in there, seemed for the first time as real as the rest of the world.

Part II
(1982 – 1983)

10.

Who says that you grow up without noticing it? That the process is invisible until at a certain point you realize you've changed? Maybe it's like that for guys. For girls, no, there's at least one precise moment for each of us, which isn't a slow and imperceptible transition but a sudden and concrete event, traceable to a second of a minute of an hour of a day of a precise year. It's the second when your blood begins to come out of you, just like that, on its own, without a wound, without a warning.

For me, that passage coincided with a moment that I will never forget, as if my life had planned to give me a climactic scene to let me know that I was no longer a child. Perhaps because it knew that I would have resisted leaving childhood with all my strength, and that outgrowing my clothes from the previous year wouldn't be enough to convince me that I was growing up.

When Caterina finished middle school, no one doubted that she should enroll in *liceo classico*, the Classics high school. In Giglio there were no high schools. My mother was keen on moving out with her. We would rent a place in Orbetello for the whole winter and then, once tourist season began, she and Vittorio would commute back and forth. They would alternate, and Nonnalina would help them until the beginning of summer vacation. The plan was doable and my mom was happy at the prospect of returning to the *continent*, to a new life with some surprises, the movie theatre, new encounters, shops, some short trips that didn't require ferries, and the recovery of the smallest amount of privacy, which was impossible on the island.

But Caterina insisted on going to boarding school: "Why should you all have to follow me? I'm not the head of the household, why should we uproot Teresa? She has to finish middle school here, how will the hotel manage with you gone for six months, moving the whole family is too expensive, and who will watch the dogs?" She finally said, "Mom, you can't stand me, wouldn't you feel a sense of liberation if I left by myself? That way you can finally enjoy your favorite daughter in peace without any outbursts of jealousy." My mother didn't want to hear it. Vittorio, who seemed to have little say in the final decision but wasn't entirely against the idea of boarding school, accidentally found a way to convince Elena.

He insisted to Caterina that boarding school was a nightmare. It had been for him, when he had gone to board in Pisa for years, taught by priests, from middle to high school, and he recounted the horror of the dormitory, of the long distance from home, the embarrassment of going out, even when he was already a young man, lined up two-by-two behind the priest, two afternoons a week. He asked Caterina how an insubordinate pain-in-the-ass like her thought she would squeeze into a place where the most important thing is the rules, followed by respect for the rules, and thirdly, ironclad discipline. He laughed. "For someone who didn't learn to read the clock until she was 10 because she didn't need it . . . I'd love to see you when they time even the five minutes you have to go to the bathroom." Then came the nail in the coffin: "I'll send you there—in my opinion it will even be quite good for you, but I bet five hundred thousand lire that by Christmas break you'll have already made Mommy come pick you up and bring you back home."

He shouldn't have challenged the two of them like that.

Eventually, we stopped talking about it because the decision had been made. Caterina would go to Poggio Imperiale in Florence. It meant a lot to my dad that at least she wouldn't waste her intelligence at a low-level boarding school in Grosseto, shabby and neon-lit, where all the day students ended up and at sixteen years old strolled around outside smoking cigarettes between the street and Piazza Duomo, getting picked up on scooters, and growing fat on slices of pizza.

Poggio Imperiale. *Il Poggio.* It was the most elite Italian boarding school. It was a sixteenth-century villa overlooking Florence with frescoes on the ceilings, a chapel, and a park with fountains. The boarding school where generations of noble ladies and lords from half of Europe had studied. A place that, when one evening Caterina finished reading aloud the informational brochure that came in the mail, my mom summarized as: "The typical place one enters as a snob and leaves insufferable—I get it." But Vittorio was happy, Caterina excited, my mom defeated, and I desperate.

In the days before her departure, Caterina promised me that I could sleep in her bed with her. Her last night at home I couldn't sleep. I tossed and turned between the sheets and at a certain point Caterina asked me to get out: we had to sleep because in the morning we would have to get up early to catch the first ferry. I sat down next to her.

"Cate, I wish you won't leave."

She stayed silent, holding herself back from correcting my grammar.

"I know that you'll come back and we'll be together for the summer, but you're leaving me all alone. I don't want to be here without you. And now I feel like crying and so I'm going to cry. But you have to sleep so I'll leave you alone."

I went to my bed. In the dark, from across the room, she replied.

"Come on Teresa, don't be so dramatic! Think about me, I'll be all by myself there too, I won't know anyone and you'll all be far away."

"You were the one who insisted on going to boarding school."

"I don't know if it was actually a good idea."

"Are you crazy? Then don't go! You still have time. Tell Mom and Dad tomorrow and we won't go."

"I can't."

"Why?"

"Because then I would ruin everything. I would lose the bet. They'll think I was a total brat for no reason, and that I made them waste money on the registration too. It's a lot of money. They'll make me pay for it forever. And there's no alternative since school starts in three days. They already hate me. Imagine if I tried to take it all back . . ."

"They who?"

"Mom and Dad."

"That's not true, they don't hate you."

"I only get along with you."

"Same for me."

"No, Teresa, you get along with everybody. Don't worry. Everything will be fine. Now go to sleep, it's late."

"You'll make new, older, and smarter friends, and I won't matter to you anymore."

"I don't believe that. I bet I'll be disliked by everyone, like always."

"Not everyone dislikes you. I don't. Don't leave."

"I can't. And don't whine about it, please."

That morning, when Mom came to get us at 5:30 A.M., she found us curled up together in my bed.

It was one of those classic departures, full of goodbyes. With the heavy suitcases, and Nonna, who had prepared sandwiches for the trip, and Irma, who had been whining inconsolably since dawn, all four of us were together in a way we hadn't been since even before I was born. Then came the sea crossing and the highway and the feeling of disorientation that always hits me in the city: the traffic lights, the traffic, the sound of sirens that terrifies me, all those artificial lights that I'd never seen before. The certainty of not recognizing anything familiar there and the added fear of being in Florence, the city of the serial-killer Monster that we'd all heard about. From every car, every bush, every tree, a horrendous being, a morbid and cruel man could suddenly appear, capable of doing terrible things, especially to the bodies of girls.

The hill of Poggio Imperiale could easily have been one of his hiding spots. A long driveway lined with cypresses, an isolated villa surrounded by box hedges, and an abundance of secluded corners in the huge, gravel-covered garden. Even though it was a place of placid and reassuring beauty, I expressed this thought.

"Couldn't it be that the monster's around here?"

My mother shot back: "Great, Teresa, you've been whining since this morning. According to you, we brought you with us to season everything with tears and terror, because we do not have enough of it already, isn't that right?" Vittorio spun it his way: "Don't worry, Teresina. First of all, the monster only kills in the fields at night, and at boarding school you can't go out at night. Second, he kills only couples, and we know that with her temper, Caterina will be forty before she finds a boyfriend that she can be with, and the monster will already be dead and buried by then."

"Thanks, Dad," replied Caterina, "It's really nice to know that you're appreciated by your own parents. In moments like this you guys are really reassuring. A fantastic family. I want to think that you're doing it on purpose so I won't miss you."

I continued to deny her accusations, blubbering on that I was only worried for her.

We parked our dull Volvo among the metallic Mercedes. Dad took the suitcases into the lobby while Mom was already dealing with an instructor who would show us the dormitory, the cafeteria, the library, and the banquet hall. Everything scared me: the super high ceilings, the stuccoes, the crystal chandeliers, the hallway full of busts, the coldness of that vastness. And the grey uniforms, the instructor who smiled but you knew they were bitches, all those blonde girls, who were secure thanks to their Naj-Oleari trunks and blue moccasins. I was happy that I didn't have to stay, but knowing that Caterina would be left there made my stomach churn anyway. The intelligent part of me would remain there, my partner in crime, the evil half, the brilliant half, the most loved half, she who loved me, and whom I would always miss.

After the visit we had lunch at a random restaurant not far from the school. I could barely eat anything. Caterina spent the lunch filling a paper napkin with drawings. When the check came she said the napkin was for me. It was covered with magnificent flowers that intertwined with one another, a drawing of us two with Irma, scenes of Giglio with hearts where clouds should have been, a big villa quite similar to Poggio surrounded by threatening lightning, and a small Heidi at the feet of a gigantic Miss Rottenmeier. I felt a terrible pain in my stomach. Before we left I asked to go to the bathroom. Mom was shaking, she told me to hurry up. She made Caterina go with me. She held the door for me so I wouldn't have to lock it. Once I got inside that cramped bathroom, which smelled like a bleach-soaked and never-dried rag, I saw a dark red spot in the middle of my underwear. I sacrificed half of the napkin that my sister had drawn on to dry the blood and protect my panties.

From outside, Caterina told me to hurry up. I didn't say anything. I pulled up my pants and left in a hurry.

Back in Giglio, it wasn't as if I'd become an only child but rather an orphan. I went to school, did my homework, watched cartoons, and I felt alone.

Though I tried to remind myself of the psychological tortures that my sister had inflicted upon me, I was mired in the void of sadness that was left without her stories, her ruthless ways, her emotional manipulation. No one could replace her. When they were home, Mom and Dad fought. Without Caterina there, they took it out on one other. I didn't understand the reasons behind those fights. Hearing them scream scared me and I felt even more abandoned. I would hide in my room and, with my head under the pillow, I read and reread the letter my sister had sent me from Poggio in which she told me about her first few days.

> *Dear Teresina,*
> *Don't tell Mom and Dad but being here is a nightmare. I'm in a four-person dorm where it's practically impossible to sleep. My bunkmate, Diana (who insists you say her name with the English pronunciation), is from Manciano (and so we'll surely see her in Giglio), and she snores like a wild boar. Across from us are the Piccolotti twins, two identical Sienese aristocrats named Chiara and Caterina, like the saints. They're blonde, thin as twigs, incredibly nerdy, and competitive. You can only tell them apart because one always cries at night and the other one doesn't, so in the morning I know which one is Caterina because she has red, swollen eyes. School is challenging. There are twenty of us in the class: ten from the boarding school and ten day students. Among the day students, there's one from the Pucci family, Ludovica, the Ludo (here we put an article in front of our names, like you do with things), whom by the first day of school I already wanted to beat up. Then there's one who wears a silk scarf at fourteen years old and talks about Alì, her Arabian horse,*

with whom she does a mysterious activity called dressaasg.
*I've started Latin, Greek, and even German. By the evening
my brain is fried, and once a week after homework they take
us to CHOIR (bleeeh) which I hate. I have terrible pitch, and
I just open and close my mouth so it looks like I'm singing.
Then there is athletics, but for now I'm not signed up for anything. I only put my name down for the activity. Getting to
Know Florence. That way maybe they'll take me out of this
prison every so often. Then there is the instructor who is a
kind of anxious mother who doesn't even love you. They
come into your room at 7:00 A.M., eat with you, watch how
you hold your fork or your pen, and yell at you if you're sitting hunched over or slouched. My Histy (the nickname
comes not from* instructor *but from* hysterical*) is a first-rate
bitch and it's already obvious that she hates me. The other
night at dinner she stopped me from taking two servings of
the first course. I'm always hungry. I'm used to Nonnalina's
portions and after having studied all day long I want to have
a second plate of lasagna. She told me, "You can't have two
servings of pasta. We keep an eye on everyone's waistlines
here. You don't want to get fat." I couldn't resist and I said to
her, "Are you worried you'll have to lend me your clothes?"
She gave me detention and I couldn't go to the TV room in
the evening for a week. Who gives a shit, anyway? The
evening TV sucks so I read and try to fall asleep before the
wild boar goes to bed.*

*I got an A on one of my assignments for History. Tell Mom
and Dad only about that, that I'm clever, I'm studying, and
I'm fine. Also write to me from that asshole of an island, you
little bitch. Actually, in Florentine dialect they say arsehole.*

Ciao!

I read and reread it. When the time came to write her back
I froze. I didn't know what to tell her about, and what I wrote

always seemed so boring. After three or four drafts that I threw away, I decided to send her a package with some cookies from me and Nonnalina along with a postcard that said: *Here at the* arsehole *everything is fine, everything's the same, I can't wait for you to get back, write me again about what you're doing and about the other girls at the boarding school. I miss you.*

11.

After Christmas vacation, which was an endless sequence of stories, games, food, and arguments inside a bubble of just me and Caterina, when she left for school again I fell ill. I ate little, never wanting to get out of bed, and I would have willingly gone into hibernation until summer and the return of life on earth.

After my third relapse my parents called the doctor. She was new and she looked very beautiful to me, like almost all new things that came to my world from outside. She visited me with a smile and said that it wasn't anything serious, but I had slightly swollen lymph nodes on my neck, and she advised my mother to have me tested for mononucleosis. Her suspicion was correct. From that moment on she was part of our household. Her name was Alice, our Trojan horse.

I had to keep my white blood cell count under control and stay home from school for quite some time. Every week I had to get a blood test. Alice would come to collect my samples at home and every time she would bring me a little prize for my bravery: a flower, a pack of trading cards, a chocolate. She would almost always come on Tuesdays in the mornings, when she didn't have to go to the clinic and so could stay a bit longer. She would sit on my bed and, while she prepared the tourniquet and test tube, she'd tell me about all sorts of things to distract me. That moment was so beautiful to me, even with the smell of the disinfectant, the pinch of the needle, and the black blood rising in the syringe. Often, before leaving, Alice would have a coffee and chat with my mom, who towards the end would ask her what time she finished at Campese that night and tell her to come back to our house afterwards. So in the evenings Alice would return. She would come to my room with me and we would read stories together. She brought me my first horror books: together, we read Lovecraft and then Stephen King. We would lie side by side on my bed and read two pages each, until it was half past nine. The stories didn't really scare me, but it was nice to pretend. We snuggled under the comforter, the two of us, with the thrill of secrecy. I waited for that moment, and if the wind whistled outside it was made even more beautiful. One evening while we were finishing "The Last Rung on the Ladder" my dad came into my room.

In a soft voice he said, "Teresa, maybe you should read by yourself. You won't always be able to kidnap Alice for hours. You're already eleven years old. Do you know how many times she's said that she would come to Castello and instead stayed here with you?" Alice replied that it was her pleasure and there had been no kidnapping. I waited for Dad to leave, but he didn't. "Come on, Alice, we're going out tonight. Teresa, it's time for you to go to sleep." He took the book out of Alice's hands, dog-eared the page and placed it on the nightstand. She got up. He tucked me in, gave me a kiss on the forehead, and they both left, turning off the light. I kicked the sheets—I couldn't stand feeling stuck and I would always sleep with a leg uncovered. I thought that if he had tucked me in like that, my father must have never seen me sleeping. I struggled to fall asleep. After that, Alice and I read together only two more times. Then she lent me the books, and I kept reading by myself.

On our last evening, she told me that she wanted children and hoped that if she had a girl, that she would be like me. I was happy. It seemed to me that I could learn so many things from her, including not to be afraid of sweetness, which in my house seemed to be lacking more and more.

Since Caterina had left, I spent more time with Mom and Dad. Whereas before they had been supporting characters, now they were center stage and I, for the first time, had the opportunity to observe them. They never touched each other and it was difficult for them to address one another with kindness. I would look at them and measure the distances, the trajectories created by their movements when they were in the same room. Their bodies only came close by accident. They tended to keep a lot of space between them.

One afternoon, Pietro and I decided to go down to the rocks behind the green lighthouse and gather limpets. We brought plastic bags and he carried an extra diving knife for me. Rosa, Pietro's mom, used to make a sauce with the limpets, which, according to Pietro, was the best thing in the world. The limpets were easy to remove and there were a lot of them. I was skillful with the knife, which was flat on one side and serrated on the other. A small tap with the tip of the blade was enough to separate the shells from the rock, but I had to make sure I grabbed them quickly with my free hand so they wouldn't slide to the bottom of the sea. Pietro resurfaced to take a breath and I passed him the bag to put his limpets in, fatter than those that I would get. At a certain point he resurfaced yelling "An octopus! I caught an octopus!" I jumped, terrified, and cut my right index finger on the knife, sideways under the nail.

"Shit! Shit! Pietro! You made me cut myself!"

He got out of the water and flung the octopus in the bag.

"Jesus Christ, I knew it, girls don't know how to fish, they always get hurt!"

He kept cursing as he helped me put on my shoes.

Without saying anything else, we ran to the doctor's office. The waiting room was empty, so we went straight into the office without knocking. Alice was there with my father. They were standing next to each other behind the desk, close to the window. All four of us stopped for a moment. Then I ended the embarrassment by opening my bleeding left hand and showing Alice my sliced finger. At that point she blushed.

She made me lie down on the bed and told me to hold my finger up and stay calm. The wound was not very deep but it needed to be treated well with a tight bandage. In the meantime, I was watching my dad standing by the foot of the bed, eyes down, while I kept my finger pointed upright. "I just came to get some suture thread," he said.

Then, he walked over and looked at my wound that was dripping blood on my palm, down my arm, and on the floor. "I would give her a stitch, wouldn't you, Alice?" he said.

Alice shook her head. "Let's try this. Our little girl has quick platelets: you'll see that the wound heals fast."

Then she turned toward him. "She lost a bit of blood. I suggest a hearty meal this evening."

"Would you like to come over?"

"No thank you, you should be together as a family tonight."

Among the reasons that I would have wanted to turn back time to the beginning of that day was not only my wounded finger but also Alice's strange rejection of the dinner invitation knowing that I would have preferred that she come, and then those compassionate looks and fake victimization and "our little girl" and a feeling of annoyance, of disappointment that I couldn't place and could only attribute to the wound.

We made our way home with Babbo in silence. He didn't say anything until we were at the door. "The whole reason I went to the doctor's office was to get the thread and then you arrived and I forgot it."

"Go back and get it then."

"It doesn't matter, I'll go tomorrow," he sighed. "Tell Mama that it's nothing serious."

"Sure. Just a little scratch."
Babbo, Babbo. What are you doing?

At home Mama scolded me weakly, telling me that I had to stop going around and hurting myself with that reckless Pietro. Afterwards she said, "Here's something you'll like," and pulled a letter out of her purse that had arrived from Florence. I kept it under my plate until the fruit course, enjoying the pleasure of anticipation. After dinner I had something sweet to enjoy in solitude. It was a blue envelope and inside there were two sheets of lined notebook paper with punched holes.

> *Dear Teresaccia,*
> *You can't even imagine how happy I am that school is ending. I'm counting the days down on the calendar—actually, I X them out with a cross in the evening, like a prisoner. I'm going to have a hell of a week coming up, three exams: Latin, Greek, and Math, and three oral tests, History, Greek, and Italian. I study all day long, under Histy's evil eye. Now that the school year is almost finished and I won the bet with Babbo, I can say that for the most part he was right: boarding school, as much as they try to pass it off as a cool, luxurious, and elite place, is little more than a prison. Sure, now I know how to eat grapes with a knife and fork, which will come in very handy in life, especially when I'm in the insane asylum and they give me a knife to eat fruit with, which I'll use to cut my wrists. Just kiddinggg. But I really can't stand it anymore. Every night, I dream of Giglio and of being with you on a boat, on the beach with Irma, eating spaghetti alla pirata, or even the evenings in Castello's moldy cellars. Everything seems better than being here and sometimes, when I wake up in the morning and have anxiety about going to school, I wish I were Nonnalina, and envying a person who is 75 years old is not great. The competition is tough so, Teresa, prepare*

yourself, because you'll go through it too. You know, coming from a place like Giglio doesn't help you any. We'll always have to try twice as hard as other people to not seem like troglodytes. Eventually I became good friends with Diana the Boar. At least we're both from Maremma and share a taste for good food in large quantities. Her family in Manciano has two or three restaurants and I can't wait to try them. She tells me all the good things they cook . . . here they feed us very little, as cellulite doesn't befit a young woman from Poggio. I'm sorry to hear that Babbo and Mama "haven't been getting along." From what I can read between the lines, through your usual way of sweetening the truth, they probably fight daily. By the way, hurray for Stephen King, I also like him a lot. See you so sooooooon. And write to me, you're lazy as an unripe fruit.

12.

When school finished, Mama and I drove to get Caterina in Florence. The trip there was unforgettable. We had never traveled just the two of us. It was clear that it was a beautiful moment for her as well. She drove in the fresh air of a June morning and I was sitting next to her. We talked about what we would do; she said after we got Caterina she wanted to take us to Principe to buy clothes if it wasn't too hot outside. I was excited to pick Caterina up and bring her back. I wanted the trip there to go by quickly. We talked about my teachers and the characters in Giglio, and I agreed with everything she said. Every so often I would fall asleep in the heat while on either side of us flew by hills ripe with wheat, sunflowers that were still closed, the withered remains of the poppies, the yellows of the clays and the dark green cypresses, the blue sky, and with all of this colorful beauty under my eyelids I looked forward to the beginning of the summer and the long break with my sister. When we passed Siena, Mama told me that we had to stop there on our way back to pick up Alice, who would return to Giglio with us. We would get some gelato in Piazza del Campo. It was a trip home with all of my favorite women. I was in a great mood.

When we arrived there was a bustle of cars and baggage. I stood in the corner to watch. I wondered if Ludo, the anorexic twins, or Diana were among the girls I saw. I observed their parents, the blue or striped shirts worn by the mothers, too, the abundance of blonde hair and gold jewelry. The wealth of those girls seemed untouchable, a promise kept since birth. When Caterina arrived I was startled. She was different from how I left her; taller, skinnier, with longer hair. She had a white shirt with the sleeves rolled up and her red hair all wavy fell onto her shoulders. Her breasts had grown. The paleness she'd earned from studying made her freckles and dark under-eye circles more evident. She was so beautiful and no longer looked like a child. I ran to hug her but she pushed me aside, saying, not now, come on. While Mama carried the brown luggage to the car, she kissed her friends goodbye and they exchanged numbers and addresses and promises to keep in touch. She didn't seem like someone who was being freed from prison and the other girls didn't seem like how she described them in her letters. From the corner, I was watching and realizing that things might not go as I'd expected.

Between goodbyes, paperwork, and meetings with the teachers, it got late. But Mama didn't want to give up on a spin around town.

"Let's go get a sandwich at Rivuar's," she said.

"Jeez, Mom, you're so lame," Caterina said.

"Let's hear what's wrong with eating and enjoying Piazza della Signoria."

"You're so obsessed with fancy places recommended by

tourist guides, where they rip you off for a piece of toast with half a slice of ham. You go to Rivoire for breakfast, buy clothes at Principe, where everything is expensive, you would go to dinner at the Pinchiorri enoteca—because these are the only places you know, places for the Americans, for people with no experience or taste."

Mama stiffened. "Perfect, we won't eat or buy anything. Both of you get in the car. We're going to Siena."

"Why are you so angry, Mama?" asked Caterina.

"Why am I so angry? Because I have a daughter who doesn't do anything besides criticize and argue and I think this school has made it worse, if that's possible."

"But who criticized? I was only saying that there are some alternatives that you don't even consider. And what does school have to do with it?"

They had already started again. I laid down on the fake brown leather of the back seat with my elbows over my ears, every so often catching words like *conceited, strict, lack of respect, but you heard yourself, exaggerated reactions, and what about you, and what about you, what about you.* Any good mood I'd felt when we left was gone.

"And who do we have to go pick up in Siena?"

I was the one to reply.

"It's Alice, the new doctor. She's nice. She's been over for dinner a bunch of times."

"Sure. The umpteenth freeloader at our house. Not only dinners, but taxi rides too. It's award-winning service."

"God, you are so bitter, Caterina. You don't even know her," I said.

When we arrived in Siena it was past one in the afternoon and scorching hot. We tried to walk under the narrow shade of the medieval buildings, following groups of foreigners that moved in packs, stunned.

When we entered Piazza del Campo, I was out of breath for a moment. The buildings and towers that bordered it in a dense grid of descents and slopes opened up to let the city breathe. The piazza was a wide open diaphragm, a huge sunny shell, full of air and light, ready to welcome anyone who wanted to lie down on its reddish interior. And lying down in the Campo was something that everyone wanted to do. My sister was looking at me. I asked her why.

"You look astonished," she told me, "that it's so beautiful."

"Are you joking?"

"No. I wish I were in your shoes. The emotion that you feel the first time you see a place like this, you never feel again."

I was about to doze off, dazed by the sun and the enchantment of the beauty, when I heard a voice whispering in my ear. *Teresinaaa . . .*

"Alice! You were right when you said that this was the most beautiful piazza in the world!" I hugged her.

After some brief shopping it was time for us to leave if we were going to catch the last ferry. On the way we began to talk about summer. Mama knew that the most difficult time of the year for her was about to start. The same was true for Alice. The population of Giglio suddenly doubled and even though they sent an assistant to help her, there was always double the patients, the injured, and the burned. Lucky you, they told us, school vacations are the most beautiful times of your life; once you start working you'll never have three months of vacation without obligations again.

Caterina responded, "Well, for us it's a real bummer. We never go on vacation like the others do. We always stay at home."

"What are you complaining about?" asked Alice. "Your house is in Giglio, a marvelous place to spend the summer. And the winter too, I'd say. People pay good money to go there on vacation, and you have the privilege of being there already. Isn't that fantastic?"

"No. It's not fantastic at all. All of my school friends have very busy plans for the summer. They're going on trips, they're going abroad, some to the mountains, some to France, some to Spain or to England, either with family or alone on a study vacation. Some of them are going to three or four different places. When they asked me what I was doing for the summer all I could say was *I'm staying home*. We've never gone on a trip the four of us, never taken a vacation. Truly, Giglio is beautiful, but it sucks. I'd like to see something else. The world is big."

"You don't realize the privilege you have," continued Alice. "I really don't understand what you have to complain about . . . you don't know how many people would give anything to live where you do."

My sister pushed her face into the space between the two front seats to make herself more audible. "It's *me*, Alice, who struggles to understand what this has to do with you. Are you trying to convince me I'm the luckiest person in the world? What do you care? I'm talking about what I'd like to do and I'm talking about it to my mother, not to you. If you like staying in Giglio and to you it's the most beautiful place in the world, stay there, no one's stopping you. But don't come and tell me how I have to feel, what to think or want. I don't even know you. What do you want from me?"

I elbowed her. Alice was about to answer, but my mother interrupted.

"Caterina, I think you're exaggerating as usual. You respond aggressively to someone who was only trying to be nice and help you see that the glass is half full. But to you the glass is not only half empty, it's broken, too. Your way of doing things is unbearable. We've been together for five hours and you already managed to fight with everyone."

"You're the ones fighting with me! You all want me to shut

up. But I'm not going to shut up. I say what I think, and everyone is bothered by my honesty. You all always lie: you lie to others and to yourselves and when someone tells you the truth or expresses a real thought you get as pissed off as if you've been punched."

"This isn't about honesty, Caterina. You pass off as honesty a habit of rubbing things in people's faces, responding rudely, complaining about everything. If it were only honesty there'd be no need to raise our voices every time."

"Actually, it's exactly the opposite! You perceive personal opinions as complaining or rudeness. The incredible thing is that everyone, even people that I don't know, automatically feels authorized to yell at me as soon as I open my mouth."

"Well, there are many ways to express opinions," offered Alice. "You might not be aware of it, but from the little I've heard it seems like you are constantly at war with the world. It seems to me that you clash with those who have no intention of wronging you. They told me that you were very different from your sister . . ."

Oh no, no.

"I see that speaking badly about me remains my family's favorite pastime, even in my absence. I'm glad. Whoever enters our house must immediately know that I am bad and Teresa is good. And if they don't understand that on their own, there's always someone ready to explain it to them. Right Tere?"

I intervened. "Not true. You're being dramatic. But Mama, could you pull over for a moment? I have to throw up."

On the ferry I felt much better, with the air on my face and the lights of the island approaching. Caterina pulled a copy of a women's magazine out of her backpack.

I got closer to her so we could read an article on summer fashion together. The things I had bought did not seem to belong to any of those categories.

I realized that her year at boarding school had been much longer than my year at home. Caterina's life had suddenly accelerated. Those three years of age difference plus her experience away from home, the splendor of her almost fifteen years, her height, long hair, breasts, everything that she had learned, from ancient Greek to how to use eyeliner, carried twice the weight. And I knew that I wouldn't be able to catch up with her in a summer, and it was as if I had already lost her. But I didn't feel defeated and I hoped I'd be able to keep up with her. I wasn't going to give up.

13.

The events of that summer made clear to me the distance that I had vaguely intuited. Caterina and I tried to keep the adults as far out of sight as possible and it wasn't difficult. Mama worked without stopping, Babbo, work or no work, was always busy with something that didn't include us. Nonnalina guaranteed us excellent meals as well as clean and ironed clothes, but it was out of the question that she would keep up with us since we were out the whole day and night with our group of friends. The group consisted of a mix of islanders and Romans, and it grew or shrank depending on whether we were on the beach or out in the evening, and on the length of the foreigners' vacations.

There were two constant elements, the alpha male and the alpha female, whom the others followed closely: Giggi, the sixteen-year-old son of the Overkills, and Caterina.

Until the year before we had never given Luigi a passing thought, and when he was little we ostracized—if not harassed—him. We never liked playing with him because he seemed stupid and dirty. But evidently that winter he had gone through a double metamorphosis: a growth spurt aided by the gym and having finally gotten his braces off. He transformed himself into an athletic young man with muscles, confidence, and fashionable clothes.

We always went to the same beach, and we were all between twelve and seventeen years old. We spent time swimming, playing cards at tables in the bar, sunbathing, and listening to cassettes on our portable stereo. We ate a ton of gelato and worried about nothing. Days made up of sweat, toned bodies, light-filled images already saturated with a type of nostalgia, on their way to becoming faded memories.

Class warfare was something we had only vaguely heard about. Our fights all took place in the same context of wealth that we all shared, but there were divisions along the lines of city versus island and male versus female. Above all, there was a much more subtle and complicated struggle that still carried with it the fear of being disliked which was disguised under a kind of arrogance.

It was time to decide what to do for Giggi's birthday, on August 22nd. For a few days we discussed two options, as if it were a government-level decision: a party on the beach, with a bonfire, barbecue, and night swim, or a party at the villa on the rocks, joining the party for his mother Desi's birthday, which was two days before, where we could take advantage of a luxurious dinner, music, and terraced gardens.

Luigi fought for the first option, saying in dialect, "No, come on, a party with old fogeys, do you really want me to have a party with my mother?"

Caterina humiliated him with pleasure: "Old fogeys? Who says that? We'd have to bring all the food with us to the beach. And how should we bring it, with the scooters, walking? I bet the police will arrive to put out the fire. You remember what happened last year, don't you? We ate raw sausages and sand. At your house we can eat, dance, and then after the cake, if we feel like it, we can still have a night swim."

"Ugh, a party full of parents, like when we were four years old?"

It was clear that the group was already on Caterina's side because there was no one who didn't want to go to dinner with the Overkills. Everyone wanted to spend a night in their mansion, which was famous for its parties, the best Roman food prepared by the two Filipino maids that they brought everywhere they went, the amount of alcohol, the dance floor they set up on the huge terrace, and the private path to the sea from its rocks that had more than once posed a risk to the overkill guests of Luigi's overkill parents.

Caterina and I were finishing recording three sixty-minute TDK tape cassettes from commercial radio stations with summer hits for the party. The songs were almost always cut off before the end, to avoid hearing the voices of the DJs.

"What are you going to wear?" I asked Caterina.

"What am I going to wear to what?"

"What do you mean to what? To the party."

"I don't know, I haven't decided yet. Maybe the little purple dress."

"Can I wear your mini skirt with the high-waisted elastic belt?"

"No, come on, I was thinking I'd wear that."

"Just a second ago you were thinking of wearing the purple dress, and now you change your mind."

"Yes."

"Now that I asked you if I could borrow it."

"Yes."

Our parents were also invited to Desi's birthday. By the time we left, we were all dressed to the nines. On the short drive we talked about the Overkills.

"What did you get Desi?" asked Caterina.

"A Roberta di Camerino scarf and a bottle of whiskey."

"Is that enough?"

"It's too much for someone who doesn't need anything."

"What does it matter, it's her birthday."

"We're bringing her a gift, at least. And I'm sure she'll appreciate it. Especially the liquid part . . ."

Vittorio chuckled.

I asked, "But what exactly does Sergio do for a living?"

"He's rich because of his family. He inherited a window and shutter factory. But they say that he makes ties too—so did his father, apparently," Babbo explained to me.

"Ah, cool, ties. Strange though because I've never seen one on him."

They all laughed except for me.

"An idiot, as usual. 'Making ties' is a way for us to say loan-sharking," said my sister.

"What's that?"

"My God, Teresa, you seem like you're not from this planet. Loan sharks are rich people who lend money to the poor illegally, with absurd interest rates, usually asking for double back what they gave you."

"So we're going to the house of these criminals."

"Oh oh, stop it everyone," said Vittorio puffing smoke out the open window. "This is just chatter. Here there are no criminals, no one's guilty, and this story does not leave this car, please, especially among you kids. Understood?"

"Understood," said Caterina. "Now it's gonna be more difficult for Teresa to admit she's in love with the son of a mob boss."

"What are you saying, you jerk!"

"Come on, Tere, it's practically tattooed on your forehead that you like Luigi. Everyone likes that fool, except for me."

"Girls, stop talking like that now—a mob boss . . . Sergio is a good person until proven otherwise."

"Oh sure, he's really respectable . . . he's a half-alcoholic asshole. But there's always a certain indulgence towards wealth. Right Vittorio?" asked my mother.

"It's not about wealth. They're our friends, we have a good relationship. I don't care to investigate what, possibly, might be true of the rumors that circulate among the envious."

"Who's envious? His best friends say those things about him. Some friends . . . I bet that you would stay friends with him even if everything was confirmed true."

"Probably so, and so what? Are mistakes contagious like viruses? Have you already put me on trial, too?"

"Great. What a beautifully superficial way to relate yourself to others. If I found out that it was true I would never want . . ."

"Well, then why are you coming to this party? You don't have to spend time with these people."

"Desi invited me. And here there are only *certain kinds of people.* I accepted out of kindness and because I don't hate going out every now and then . . . but I can't say with certainty that they're my friends, and I assure you that if these rumors turn out to be true I would no longer want . . ."

We left the car on the edge of the street to continue on foot, accompanied by a double row of torches along the path that led to the villa. Two pyramids of white and red roses welcomed us, the veranda was framed with organza curtains festooned with freesias, there were tables of all sizes filled with trays that were still covered, while the entrance to the living room revealed a horseshoe-shaped structure that was covered half with bottles and half with crystal goblets, at least two hundred of them. We were the first to arrive. The only person that welcomed us was Guido, a waiter from our hotel who was working there for the evening. On the lowest terraces some kids from our group had arrived. Sergio came out of the kitchen, with his linen shirt and khaki pants ironed to a crisp, but already drenched in sweat, with his shiny bald head, holding a glass of whiskey with ice. His gaze lingering on me and my sister, he said in dialect, "Vittorio, what a great idea to host Giggi's party here too, otherwise this house would never have seen these perky tits!" My dad laughed, but Mama did not, and Sergio added, "I'm joking Elenaaa, your tits are beautiful too!" My mother turned away and started to leave. "Vittorio, I can make your wife angry better than you can, eh!"

At that moment Alice walked in, with her long legs sticking out of her mini dress, and Mama headed towards her. We joined the other kids on the terrace below. A bunch of round tables were set up there too, and the wooden fence was covered with blue tulle and sunflowers—"A gay thing," said Giggi, "that my mother came up with." We were all very excited. There were soft drinks and an abundance of ice and food. The Filipino maid was grilling sausages while the stereo blared the songs from our cassettes at full volume and we secretly passed around cigarettes.

Desi appeared on the top floor in a light blue silk dress, low-cut over her fake breasts, which were a gift to herself when she turned forty, silver sandals, and painted nails that gleamed against the crystal glass she held in her hand. With her piercing and pretentious voice, she said, "Is everything good down there, guys?"

We raised our heads, responding as a group, smiling, yessss, applauding a bit. That afternoon Desi had given Luigi a box of twenty condoms. "Give them to the others too," she said. "I know how you all are, you're too ashamed to buy them so you take risks." A gift made in the spirit of hope on behalf of her son, but one fueled by a dramatic imagination. By "risks" Desi didn't mean getting a girl pregnant: she was talking about AIDS, which we talked about non-stop that summer: just one misstep and a few months later you became a skeleton with spotted skin before you died alone, in extreme pain. All he said was, "Come on, Mom." But he took the pack and hid it under his pillow. Ashamed to confess to his mom that not only had he never used them, but also, despite what he liked to make everyone believe, he was still a virgin, and the stories he told of his trip to Lloret de Mar and of the two German girls, one after the other, were Luca's stories, his high-school friend who got held back.

At the party he poured them out, individually wrapped, on an empty plate next to the melon, cheese, and mortadella skewers, saying with a priestly air, "Take and use them, everyone." He then disappeared into the bushes and returned shortly after, with a badly hidden bottle under his shirt, a whiskey cream stolen from the adult table. "Nobody noticed it," he said, "There were three that were still corked. They think it's gross, like watered-down wine." He poured a round of Bailey's into plastic cups over ice. The excitement spread. There was a warm breeze and Duran Duran. I thought that Luigi had beautiful eyes, a soft nose that seemed boneless, and that surely kissing him would be a beautiful feeling, and I didn't care if he was stupid, if his dad was a criminal, and his mom was Desi. While I was dancing I moved closer, but to him it was as if I wasn't even there. The cake arrived. Two tiers for eighteen kids. The Filipino maid lit the candles and we sang but Desi wasn't there. At a certain point I took a slice and pretended to throw the plate at Luigi as if it were a frisbee, shouting at him, "Think fast, Giggi!" The great thing was that I meant to pretend, but the cake really slipped off the plate and flew directly onto his shirt and everybody laughed like crazy. He was annoyed, he came up to me and said, "You're so stupid," and left to get changed and I felt very bad. Giggi returned with a clean red shirt just as the cake war was about to start, but he intervened and said, "Come on, what the fuck are you all doing, let's go swim." Someone took the scooter and almost all of us girls went on foot. Beatrice, the nice daughter of the pharmacists, put another entire bottle of whiskey cream in her backpack and we passed it around, singing. When we arrived at the beach someone had already lit a small fire. We turned off the flashlights and took off our clothes. We all walked into the water and for a moment no one said anything. There was an expanse of dark sea illuminated by the phosphorescence of the plankton which lit up with our movements. An enchanting moment. On Giggi's cue there were shouts and laughter and dives. We passed the first shoal and the water was freezing; I felt light as if that joy and exaltation had taken me out of my body and then all of a sudden I couldn't swim or breathe anymore, so I tried to get to the shore, racing to get there before I drowned, and as soon as I got to shore I vomited.

"You overdid it with the whiskey cream," Beatrice said.

"I think so," I told her, running to vomit again between the rocks. When I turned around I saw two silhouettes about sixty feet from me. They were Caterina and Luigi kissing, hugging, with water up to their waists. I breathed heavily, leaning against the rocks, waiting for my tremor to stop and for the tingling in my arms and my head to pass. But it was getting worse. I was cold. I could no longer stand up.

Pietro found me unconscious next to the rocks. I was motionless and lay down next to him for a good while as he explained the stars to me. The sidereal time, the Big Dipper and the North Star—he tried to distract me while holding my legs up so I could regain my strength.

When I felt a little bit better, I asked him if he could take me to my mom, who for the umpteenth time must have thought, seeing me arrive completely pale, that Pietro always brought trouble.

The next day there wasn't a cheerful face in my house. I woke up late, had a headache, and was very thirsty. I went into the kitchen to get something to drink and found my mother, who was on her way out, and Nonna who was very serious while drying the cups.

"How are you?" Mama asked me without looking, as she applied eyeshadow with her middle finger in front of the mirror.

"Good. Bad stomachache."

"Eat light today. Cook some rice later, you guys."

She got up, took her purse, and left, slamming the door.

I went to the bathroom, where I found Caterina brushing her teeth.

"Did you know it's almost noon?" she muttered with her mouth full of toothpaste.

"Yes, did you wake up just now too? I'm not going to the beach today."

"I'm not going either. I didn't sleep very much last night."

"I know."

"*You know* what?"

"You've been busy. Look, I saw it all."

"But what did you see, if you weren't there. You were already gone."

"What the fuck are you saying Cate, are you kidding me?"

"Let's hear it: what did you see, exactly?"

"I saw you with Luigi, don't be a fool. You kissed and held each other in the water." I imitated her: "*I don't like him, I don't like him, he's stupid, he can't speak*, but see in the end . . . look, if you think you hurt my feelings, you're wrong."

"Listen you fool, there are more important things than that idiot. We were drunk, we kissed, there's nothing between us. He doesn't even know how to kiss. I don't want to talk about it ever again. You saw me, but I saw something else, a terrible thing."

"And what would that be?"

"Well, when we got back to Luigi's, you were already gone. I went down to the terrace because I wanted a sunflower as a party souvenir. Luigi told me to, I didn't really give a shit, but I did it to make him happy, poor guy. And when I was there trying to untie the fucking sunflower, I looked down and guess who I saw kissing and petting?"

"Who?"

"Hold on tight."

". . ."

"Babbo."

"Babbo? What do you mean?"

"With your friend Alice."

"No. It's not true."

"Unfortunately it's very true. That bitch. I told you right away I didn't like her."

"Oh come on, you saw wrong. It was dark."

"I even saw too much."

"I don't believe it."

"Believe it."

". . . Maybe it was like you and Luigi, they were just drunk and there's nothing between them."

"Teresa, Jesus, wake up. They're adults, they have responsibilities. They were just drunk. Of course that's what he said. Certainly Mom's not willing to look the other way."

"You told Mama?" I yelled.

"Yes, why do you think I was awake at eight-thirty this morning? What else should I have done? Surely if you saw them you would've pretended that nothing happened, right, you coward? Your sweet friend Alice."

It was true. I had already pretended that nothing had happened. I was a coward. I wasn't ready for anything.

Babbo didn't come home for days. Mama was mad in her invisible and rigid way. She continued to live and work like nothing had happened, but within a few hours she had already made decisions that she could never take back. A few days after the party, without telling anyone, she left on the first ferry to search for a house to rent in Orbetello. She went to an agency that made an appointment for her that same afternoon to visit an apartment overlooking the lagoon. Learning that we could leave it empty to sublet it for the months of July and August accelerated her negotiations. She also stopped by the middle school and high school to enroll me and Caterina. A few hours later she made a quick inspection of the furnished house (three rooms, beautiful light, horrendous furniture, one bathroom, available immediately, perfect). She wrote a check for the deposit and they gave her the keys even though the lease didn't start until September 1st. In six hours she altered the lives of three other people in addition to her own and made it back to Giglio in time for dinner.

14.

From that moment on they stopped fighting in front of us. At that point maybe shame prevailed, as well as the desire to restore the distance between parents and children. We knew things that children shouldn't know, and they acted as if by not saying anything or shouting disgraceful things in front of us we would forget all of it.

The discovery of the truth, after all, was like a liberatory disgrace. Perhaps Mama had been waiting for something like this, she had wanted to leave for a while. She was sad, as sad as one would be over the death of a dying man. Babbo reacted badly to the news of our departure and to the fact that he was excluded from the decision, but it was clear too that deep inside of him the fact that he would remain alone in Giglio offered a taste of freedom.

The morning that Mama told us over breakfast that we would be moving to Orbetello and switching schools, I spilled my cappuccino and pretended that I had burned myself. I ran to the bathroom to cry. Then I told everyone that I wanted to be alone in my room to choose which things I'd take with me. Instead, around noon I grabbed a towel and set off on foot to Caldane without a hat, to let the scorching sun stun me, to let the thorns, myrtle bushes, and thistles scratch me. I stopped on a rock before the beach. I dove. I swam for a long time and at a certain point sank under the water. I wanted to go down, further and further, until I touched the black seagrass on the bottom. I felt overwhelmed by the desire to not return to the surface, to keep clinging to the algae until water filled my lungs, in that silence down there, compressed but light, hair swaying like jellyfish, all of that blue around. But I couldn't do it: my body rose of its own accord, my mouth quickly searching for air with a terrified breath. I remained motionless all afternoon on the rocks, getting sunburned, until the sun went behind the mountains. I got my towel and walked back home. Along the way, I stopped to carve a small section of a prickly pear with a small knife that Vittorio had gifted to me. I wrote my name. That inscription would remain there growing with the plant for quite a few years, with outlines gray and hard that couldn't be erased as the leaf grew taller and taller.

On the back road near my house I saw Alice walking in the opposite direction. I would have rather thrown myself into a bush than run into her, I would have turned around, if it wasn't for the fact that she saw me and was coming towards me. As we approached each other I didn't know where to look, I held my head low and heard confused thoughts rolling around in my empty head. I was about to enter a duel and I did not have a weapon, a horse to escape on, an accomplice to shoot the enemy from a window, or any clever phrases to say before dying. When she reached me, with her hair in a braid and the spiced perfume she always wore, she hugged and kissed me repeatedly on my cheeks and head. I remained immobile and mute while she cried and told me things that I've mostly forgotten but were meant to be excuses, pleas for forgiveness, and prayers to believe her, that she didn't want to hurt anyone, and that I, Teresa, was so important to her and she loved me and she didn't want to lose my love over anything in the world. I let her do it and couldn't react at all. Not even when she told me that there were things about adults that I might not be able to understand but that they wouldn't take anything away from me, "Because when there is love, it always adds to what already exists, it never takes away." This statement I remember, and I remember the extortion of a promise to always love each other, to which I nodded, condemning myself to acknowledge my own cowardice, my inability to reject the feelings imposed on me, and for years I relived that moment feeling a huge sense of guilt for my mother, because of which I replayed the scene over and over and insulted Alice, that bitch who destroyed my family; I told her to fuck off, and I told her that I never loved her and never wanted to see her again. And instead, in reality, with a half smile, I remained mute and just nodded yes while she spoke. I wasn't listening, and the one thing that I understood was probably the thing that was supposedly incomprehensible to my innocent mind. Alice was beautiful, sweet-smelling, with smooth and amber skin made of magnetic cells and anyone would've wanted to be touched by her hands and kissed by her mouth. I couldn't pull myself away. After all, the thing among adults that was so hard to understand was actually so simple. Attraction, the irresistibility of a body, stunning beauty that empties your head, erases your thoughts and inhibits your will. I understood Vittorio; I was like him.

The duel was irreparably lost. Not only had I surrendered to my opponent, but I also gave her permission to kill me without even asking her to spare me. I staggered home. After the shower I counted my injuries and burns. I used some cream that I found in the bathroom to treat my wounds.

15.

The afternoon to board the ferry arrived, the final day. There was a white delivery van full of boxes, books, suitcases, a wardrobe, and toys that Caterina and I didn't have the courage to abandon. But nothing I brought with me had anything to do with my life up until that moment. Outside of the house, far from the sea lights, every object, every dress, and every book lost its meaning, was stripped of memories. What I cared about most I couldn't bring with me. I left behind my room, the wind off the sea entering through the window, the light glittering on the granite, pyrite sticking to my feet, Irma the dog, the smell of the port, the smell of my smell. Those were the only true signs of my early life, which would come to a close along with the door of the Rio Marina at 3:00 P.M. on September 2nd, 1983. Before getting on the boat I did something absurd: I jumped from the dock to the beach, grabbed a handful of sand and shoved it in my mouth. I tried to swallow but only partially succeeded. I spat several times, and for a few hours afterwards I had sand grains scraping between my teeth. Once we embarked, after waving goodbye to Pietro, Pietro who stood motionless with his head lifted, I went inside the cabin and didn't look out once during the trip. My mouth had a horrendous taste and I sat in an armchair below deck, keeping my eyes closed with the hope of falling asleep. I felt seasick for the first time, and from that day forward I would always suffer from it.

The house where we went to live on the mainland didn't have a telephone. Vittorio was to call the neighbors, the Partellis, in case of an emergency. Mrs. Partelli was a promoter of the ban on hanging sheets over the balcony, because it was "Neapolitan." Their only daughter, Sonia, was thirteen, had a big nose and ass, and always dressed impeccably. She went to my school but was in eighth grade.

The evening of September 23rd, Vittorio called the Partellis asking for Elena. Sonia arrived in her bear-shaped slippers. "Ms. Elena, there's someone on the phone for you."

Mama was preparing pasta carbonara. She ran to the neighbors' house.

"Hello, Vittorio?"

"Yeah."

"What's wrong? Why are you calling at this hour? I told you a thousand times that here . . . I'm making dinner and we're disturbing the neighbors."

"Christ, you always have to argue. If I call you it's because I have something urgent to tell you. The letter from the Florence Appeals Court arrived."

"Excuse me, it arrived at 8:30 P.M.?"

"Fuck, I only just got home now, it wasn't in the hotel mail. You're so argumentative, are you interested in what it has to say or not?"

" . . . "

"Our sentence was upheld. And they made it worse. Instead of a month and ten days we were given six months. The crime of 'interruption of a public service' became 'naval blockade.' Which is much more severe. And we have to pay almost seven hundred thousand lire for the court costs."

"You're joking."

"Unfortunately not."

"I can't believe it. Is it the same thing for all thirty who were sent back to trial?"

"No, not for everyone. For us as well as for Mario, Ettore, Pietro, Giuseppe. And I also think Paola, Biagio, Tarcisio, Gino . . ."

"I'm sorry, but . . ."

"Yes, only the socialists and communists were convicted.

The Christian Democrats were acquitted. They accepted the motions from the defense that said they only participated in the blockade of the port for solidarity, for friendship . . ."

"This can't be possible."

"Yes Elena, it's possible."

She got angry.

"But do you fucking understand what this is? Does it seem possible to you that this could happen? Freda and Ventura were acquitted because of insufficient evidence and after all that, eleven years after the massacre, who gets convicted? Us, the protestors. No Vittorio, we have to take to the streets again here. It can't end like this."

"Take to the streets? What are you talking about? We have our sentence: we did block the port, after all, no? Or actually, it was you who was there . . . I wasn't even on the boat."

"What are you saying? You seem proud of the sentence."

"Of course I'm proud—I did something illegal but right, and now I'm paying for it."

"How can you say that it's okay? How? The point is that terrorists are acquitted here and meanwhile we have to do six months of house arrest!"

The Partellis began to talk under their breath while they chewed their pasta.

From the other end of the line Vittorio continued.

"Elena, do you understand that we occupy two different levels of justice? When you put it that way it seems like we've been found guilty of the Piazza Fontana massacre."

"But don't you see that at the end of the day that's actually how it is? After all the investigations and trials, we're the only ones, and I mean the only ones, who have been punished?"

Mrs. Partelli looked at Elena with a serious expression.

Elena paused for a moment, put her hand over the receiver and said, "I'm so sorry, I'm done, what happened was . . ."

Then she returned to Vittorio, "I have to go now, I'll call you tomorrow morning at the hotel."

She hung up, said thank you, excused herself, and as she was leaving she thought she heard Mrs. Partelli say, "What is this craziness? That's all we need, terrorists using our telephone."

By now our pasta was inedible.

About two weeks later at the condo board meeting, which our mother never participated in, it was decided on that it would be forbidden to receive phone calls in other people's homes and that each tenant had the duty to reserve the use of their telephone exclusively for the members of the household or for their guests, for unspecified "issues of privacy and general security." Every member of the building without a telephone would have to apply to the telephone company for a private line or they would have to use the public phone booths.

One afternoon after returning home from grocery shopping, my mother, Caterina, and I ran into Lara Partelli in front of the gate. We walked toward the main door together and she held it open with one hand to let us pass. We went inside, found ourselves all in the elevator with our heavy grocery bags and got off at the same floor, all without saying a word until we were in the hallway. At the moment when our paths finally parted, my mother turned and said, "Ah, Mrs. Partelli, I wanted to tell you that, as far as I'm concerned, you can shove your telephone up your ass."

The woman pretended that she didn't hear and quickly went into her apartment.

Once we got inside, Caterina said to me, "What the fuck are you laughing at?" And to my mother that she was crazy and wanted us to get kicked out. She said that now Sonia would speak badly about us at school and ruin our already fragile reputation. Mama responded, "Who cares." Caterina was mad all evening.

16.

Years of difficult compromises with new worlds, the outside one, containing unknown people and a strict and unimaginative school, and the inside—an abyss more than a world—that changed my thoughts, mood, and character. I clung to my studies because I didn't have anything better to do that proved how smart I was. Every good grade was an anchor that stopped, for a moment, my drift into apathy and low self-esteem, was consolation for the thick glasses I had to wear, for my sense of inadequacy. Mama dusted off her economics degree and went to work as an accountant, with the idea of eventually starting her own business. Mine and my sister's problems seemed like the only ones; we always thought of our mother as someone who didn't need anything and who was there to take care of everything we needed. I remember that, at that time, the only beautiful thing that happened to me was that Caterina, who used to study a lot for high school, told me the story of the *Iliad* in the evenings before we went to sleep. She changed the ending for me. She made Hector the victor over Achilles.

Babbo came to visit us whenever he could. But the time we spent together always ended up being a sad search for ways to fill the hours. If for some reason he couldn't come and missed a visit, I was glad.

In November, there was a disastrous weekend. It was a cold and windy Saturday, and I hoped that the ferries would stop because of the rough sea, but no. My sister was in an exam period so she had to stay home and study. I had to spend Saturday afternoon alone with Vittorio. And I didn't want to at all. Our normal distance from one another became a detachment without nostalgia to me. I didn't miss him and perhaps he knew it; maybe he suffered because of it or felt the same way—I never understood him. I was no longer his devoted daughter who helped him fix the fishing hooks in the cork on the boat, who fell asleep curled up under his arm, who waited for him to take me on a ride to the port on the cart. And I hadn't even turned into a rebellious adolescent, in conflict with my father figure. We were two strangers bound by a blood bond and a sense of duty that forced us to love each other: we tried with hypocrisy.

He came to pick me up after school and we spent a good half-hour driving around in the car, listening to the music charts on the radio to fill the silence. He asked me where I wanted to go and I responded, "I don't know, wherever you want." He took me to visit some friends who had a restaurant in Manciano, whom I later discovered were the parents of Diana the Boar, who was with Caterina at Poggio. We ate around two. Everyone was smoking cigars and laughing at jokes that didn't make me laugh, not because I didn't understand them, but because they were just crude and not funny. They asked my father how Alice was and he responded laconically with glances that were meant to be intimidating. They shouldn't have asked him about her when I was there. Didn't they understand the need to be discrete on the subject? I just pretended like I didn't hear and didn't notice my father's embarrassment. Later he took me to Cala Galera to see the boats. We didn't know what to talk about. He asked me about school and I replied, "Good, I'm getting great grades," as if that said it all, because it was impossible to bridge that gap of our unshared daily lives, because I wasn't able to explain to my father that the success I achieved in school took effort, that I was afraid of being judged, and that the competition among my classmates made me ill, that being thirteen years old was so horrible that every Sunday night, when I heard the theme song of the Sunday sports recap on TV and I still had ten pages of history left to read, I wrote a suicide note. I had a diary full of them. From time to time I would address the letter to a recipient who in my mind should be crushed by a feeling of guilt and, therefore, there was one for everyone: for the bad teacher, for my classmate Debora who considered herself so cool and spoke badly about me behind my back, for my mother who had a distorted idea of who I was, for my father who minded his own business, for my sister who didn't help me enough, for Pietro who didn't respond to my letters and wasn't a true friend.

But to Vittorio none of this existed, I was only a nice young girl who was good at school and must not have had any problems. I couldn't make him believe otherwise. He was the one with problems.

As he drove he seemed to talk to himself, occasionally shaking his head. At a certain point, I asked him, "What are you thinking about?"

He replied, "Do you really want to know?"

" . . . "

"This month I didn't make any money. Do you understand? Nothing. The hotel will be closed for another three months and I'm living off of two hundred thousand lire in savings. This summer our profit went up in smoke, between the chefs and the employees. Being a veterinarian in Giglio is a useless profession. I treat a dog every two weeks and I don't ask for anything. I have two hundred thousand lire, understand? Not even enough for gas to drive you around!"

"Then let's not drive the car. We didn't have to . . ." I said in a faint voice.

"I was only saying it to make you understand how I live, Teresa. I can't go on like this: it's a shit life, you all are far away and I'm alone there and I don't know how to make you understand there are no prospects. Your mother wants her share and without money nobody can do anything. Nothing."

I don't know if it was intentional or not, but his outburst

of self-pity made me feel bad for him. We ended the afternoon in a stationary shop in Orbetello where he wanted to buy me a fountain pen. I didn't want it. I thought about the two hundred thousand lire and I couldn't justify spending ten thousand like that. As I passed along the shelves I realized that I really had to pee. I had held it in all afternoon because I was ashamed to tell him. Why was I so timid and detached that I couldn't ask him to stop because I really had to go? All I know is that I asked the shopkeeper if they had a bathroom and when she told me yes, but it was broken, I peed my pants in the doorway before running to look for a cafe. And then I cried and hid in the hood of my duffle coat and while Vittorio took me home and assured me that it could happen to anyone, I didn't utter another word.

My father and I only managed to talk about that period many years later with the help of selective memory, my suffering out of focus. And so we never confronted each other, terrified as we were of depth.

The following day I was able to convince Caterina to come to lunch with Vittorio. He would bring us home early to do our homework and would take the ferry at three. What a relief.

We returned to Manciano, to the family of Diana who took advantage of Caterina's presence to try to convince her parents to withdraw her from Poggio and send her to high school with her in Orbetello.

"It's not even a discussion," responded her mother, with her well-known Maremma savoir-faire. "In Orbetello they're all thugs: we need to give you a serious education."

Obviously Caterina couldn't pass up the opportunity.

"If you really want to know, the only thing that's more serious in Poggio than in Orbetello is the way they use their silverware. But it seems like that's what you care about most, right?" she said, waving her fork in circle to indicate the restaurant.

Vittorio gave a crooked smile and asked for information about the wine he was drinking.

When the tiramisu came Babbo told us that he had to give us some bad news. Caterina commented, "If it's that you and Mama are getting a divorce, we already know."

"No, it's not that."

". . ."

"Irma died."

"That's not true!" I yelled and then stopped talking.

"Why didn't you tell us before?" asked Caterina.

"I didn't want to say it . . ."

"How did it happen?"

"She was hit by a car near Arenella. Giuliano and your friend Pietro found her, loaded her on the Ape Piaggio, and brought her to me."

"And what did you do?"

"I buried her."

"Where?"

"Under the fig tree, in the garden."

"But what was Irma doing in Arenella alone? She had never gone up there."

"I don't know what to tell you, Cate. After you left she started running away. Every evening I would have to go look for her. Several times I found her in Cannelle. She was bored. And I couldn't keep up with her all day."

"And when you found her did you beat her?"

"I yelled at her, of course. She had to understand that she shouldn't run away."

"   "

"But I'll get you both another, okay? Aldo's setter is pregnant. Or we can get a puppy of your choosing."

Caterina responded: "We don't want a puppy, we don't want one! Besides, Babbo, I don't think we'll ever go back to Giglio. You weren't even able to take care of a dog. The day in which we understand who you care about besides yourself, when we understand if there is a crumb of love left over for anyone else in that dry heart, it will be too late."

She got up from the table and left the restaurant.

I didn't know what to do. I didn't know if I was more in despair over Irma's death, my sister's violence, or my father's humiliation. My eyes filled with tears and I wished I was somewhere else, anywhere but there, in front of a dessert that I couldn't even touch, in front of that man who held curses between his teeth and whose life, it was clear, wasn't going at all the way he wanted.

I didn't speak again all afternoon.

When it was time for Babbo to leave he came back twice to say goodbye to me after we had already closed the door.

Then I wrote to Pietro.

Dear Pietro,

My father told me that you and Giuliano found Irma dead. Why didn't you tell me? You are an asshole. I tell you this as an oath. I don't want to have a dog ever again. And I swear I'll never get one for my kids when they grow up. I swear on Irma. Can you please put flowers under the tree where Babbo buried her? Thank you. I hope that you'll write back soon. It's boring here, school is hard, and the mosquitos aren't gone yet.

A week later I received an ill-written response in which he said:

Dear Teresa, I found your dog in the middle of the road, across from Castello, past Arenella. I was on Giugliano's Piaggio Ape. Somebody ran over her, I think it was the bus. I threw her in the woods below, and then I told your dad. So I don't think there's anything under the fig tree. I didn't tell you because you would cry. I'm sorry but I don't know what she was doing up there. Maybe she went to look for you all.

The last bit tore me apart. Irma crushed by a bus, Irma thrown into the woods. Irma, with whom we couldn't play anymore. Everything was already at the limits of being tolerable, but the thought of her lost, walking for miles on the only road there was to look for us because we weren't there anymore, because we'd abandoned her—no. That was an unbearable thought.

PART III
(1999)

17

It was the first days of the last March of the millennium. In Rome, winter was over. The sun, lighter jackets, pollen, and sneezes. I felt the usual desire to run away, to have a horizon. But I stayed put, still and nervous because of my immobility. Then one afternoon I received a telegram from Paris. A thing of the past. It said, "A comfortable, smooth, reasonable, democratic non-freedom prevails in advanced industrial civilization. Escape to the sea while you can."

It wasn't signed, but only Caterina would have sent it to me. Its content, form, origin, total coherence. We hadn't spoken in a while. I called her, lying about the fact that I had understood her quote and thanking her for the originality of her invitation, but saying that it really wasn't a good time. The fact was, whether out of my habit of responding to Caterina's commands or maybe a strange sixth sense, I felt an urgency to go to Giglio. As if it were an opportunity that I'd never have again. I found the courage to ask for two days off at a time when we had four qualitative research studies underway. I had been working for over four years at Rome Marketest, a medium-sized company specializing in market research and marketing strategy managed entirely by women. I received a job offer a few months after I graduated from Bocconi with a thesis on statistics. I immediately accepted: the move to Rome after five years in Milan was a great opportunity for me. But I hated my job. With a degree in Economics and Business, I already knew what I was getting myself into, and I was prepared for a professional destiny without even a hint of passion. But I couldn't stand marketing. I didn't care at all about the goods or the companies that turned to us to increase their sales by creating products that were tailored to people's needs. I didn't believe that we were the ones who understood people's needs—if anything we had to create fake needs, which I considered fundamentally immoral. Days and days of training to pretend that the questions I asked of the focus group made sense: "If this detergent were an animal, what animal would it be?" It was a daily strain to convince myself that there was at least some truth in what I would say to a marketing director, that customer satisfaction could be hiding in packaging that was more yellow. The only justification I had was the paycheck, which allowed me to pay rent and live alone in the city. But the salary wasn't enough to fulfill me. In Rome I was content; I walked around, went out for dinner, sat in traffic and looked at the monuments, always in a hurry, and met interesting people. But there was no larger purpose to anything I was doing.

For a few months I'd been using the expression, "I really need to unplug." Every time I said it, as I finished saying the syllable "plug" and my colleagues nodded or made a joke, I felt as if the plug I was talking about was stuck in my side and my cheeks would flush with shame over what I had become: an office worker who complained about the lack of time. I was like everyone, I forgot how to manage my days, and with them weeks and months had turned into years in the office, meals eaten standing up, half-hours looking for parking, hours talking to people who had nothing to say. I was a landfill seagull, like all the greedy seagulls who leave the sea to go rummaging among the garbage bags thinking they'll find more food.

Caterina had been living in Paris for over 10 years by then.

In January of '86, after enrolling at the Florence School of Architecture and seeing what little was enough to confirm her biases about the disorganization and backwardness of Italian universities, she announced that just after her eighteenth birthday she was moving to France. Nothing would stop her. She studied French, prepared for the entrance exam to the École des Beaux-arts, passed without any problems and began her life between the Île-de-France and Maremma. She wouldn't change her mind. She ran a contemporary art magazine and was engaged to a Swiss sculptor who was highly esteemed and equally an asshole.

After Caterina's departure, Red threw herself even more into her work. She had opened an accounting office in Orbetello which was now well underway. The most important entrepreneurs in the area turned to her. She had three employees and every time we saw each other she conveyed to me, without asking explicitly, that if I came to help her it would be of great benefit to both of us and I would certainly be paid better than I was at Marketest. She lived alone with Nonnalina. She never thought about looking for another partner. She didn't want anyone interfering with her life and her choices. She'd had a long enough relationship with a bank director whom she never introduced us to. Then they relocated him to the Sardegna branch and it ended there without any regrets.

When Caterina came home from Paris for the first time, for summer vacation, one afternoon we were seated at a bar in Piazza Garibaldi, watching the muscular bodies of the young men of Orbetello go by, and she told me, "Teresa, you have to move away too. Finish this shitty high school, come with me, we'll get a beautiful duplex together in Mouffetard. You can enroll in a university and study something easy like journalism or languages, because in France the humanities are bullshit, you can start writing, you're so good, maybe you become a correspondent for an Italian newspaper, make a ton of international friends and tell this shitty place to go fuck itself. Huh, Tere?"

"Sure, sounds good, but I still have two years until I graduate."

That plan was the description of a dream.

My graduation year finally arrived. And my sister's idea deflated on its own. In the meantime she had moved lightyears ahead. She shared an apartment with a designer, continued with the École des Beaux-arts, and at the same time she began to collaborate with an art magazine for which she wrote brief reviews of young and promising artists, always getting her predictions right; she had a Spanish boyfriend, and she didn't miss me that much. She repeated, each time more weakly, that there would always be a place for me, without insisting. In the meantime, my math teacher had spoken with my father and convinced him that I should take the test for Bocconi, that surely at graduation I would have the top scores in the class, or close to them, that I had an aptitude for science and that I was a student who could face any challenge, and therefore it was worth going to a prestigious, cutting-edge university that would open me up to formidable career opportunities. Vittorio believed her. He talked to my mother and for the first time in years they agreed on something. It was 1989 and Milan was still the mirage that it had been for the whole decade that was about to end.

And it was in that very important moment that Caterina was not by my side. I found myself faced with a choice, then obeying what was asked of me because that was the way I was used to choosing, and for the first time in my life she wasn't there to give me orders. The orders came from someone who theoretically was more entitled to do so, but who had always missed the facts. It was my father who showed me the way. And in my fatal automatic compliance, I gave up all my international dreams, the European journalism schools, the house in Paris with Caterina.

That was the real moment of separation between us, when I opted for Milan. The summer after graduation my father said to everyone, "In October Teresa will go to Bocconi," and while it filled his mouth with satisfaction, I interpreted Bocconi in a literal sense of the word wich is "mouthfuls," convinced that I would be torn apart and eaten in pieces. And I wasn't totally wrong.

So, on a Thursday morning at the end of that Roman winter, I got in my car and left. It seemed to me that I didn't have much time and that everything that was most dear to me was somewhere else.

Tuscany was the usual triumph of blue skies, white clouds, and green hills of wheat. Postcards. The whole way I sang songs about rebellion that Red had taught me. I didn't tell her anything, otherwise she would have forced me to stop over in Orbetello.

When I asked for a one-way ticket at the ticket office in Porto Santo Stefano, I realized that I had lost my voice. On the half-empty ferry I looked out to see the silhouette of Giglio protruding from behind the Argentario. I fell asleep on a bench at the stern, in the sun, with newspapers under my head, dark sunglasses, and a jacket as a blanket. The mooring operations woke me up with their ever identical sounds, but I remained immobile there with my eyes closed. A crew member shook my shoulder and said to me, "Move, you need to get off, we're about to leave again. Do you want to go back?" I smiled at him without responding—I knew this grizzled bosun who treated me badly, like a tourist. His name was Angelo and I knew well the details of an event from his childhood. When he was twelve years old he injured himself with a fishing gun and they took him to my father, to treat the gash on his arm. Even though Babbo was a veterinarian, everyone trusted him more than the old doctor. Angelo cried the whole time, chirping *ow ow* in a painful little voice, identical to that of wounded hunting dogs. Surely I was the only one who remembered this detail. I was four or five years old. I was shocked by the blood and the purple swollen arm in between the black stitches. I also envied him because big scars gave guys a lot of prestige. There, on the ferry, I wanted to say to him, "Oh, Angelo, doesn't your wound hurt now that the weather is changing?" but I was a stranger to him—maybe he would have taken it the wrong way and I would have to explain who I was, and explain how I knew these things. I was no longer from Giglio, maybe I had never been, because even when I lived there I was the daughter of foreigners. With the passing of the years and my prolonged absence I found it harder and harder to be recognized. I changed a lot. But there was something more that has to do with my nature. Everyone remembered Caterina, a redhead, who looks like my mama; me, if I'm not with her, I could be anyone. There is an undefined clarity in me. If I change my haircut and wear a pair of glasses I have to explain who I am to people I've always known. I don't care. In fact, I like to go unnoticed. During my time at the university in Milan, my friends sent me to steal bottles in crowded wine bars, and indeed I would enter and leave with a Barbera under my coat, and no one would notice anything. I believe that this is really my most characteristic trait: lack of a clear outline. Perhaps it's something I have in common with islands, like the slipping away of the water and the changing landscape in the wind.

As I descended from the ferry I saw Pietro holding his son by the hand. I was surprised how big the little boy had become and how identical he was to his father at that age. I have a square, reddish photo from the early seventies, in which we're together on the kindergarten swing, and he was exactly the same child with dark eyes who at that moment was watching cars exit from the mouth of the ferry.

18.

Pietro and I had known each other since we were little kids. Our friendship started to unravel after I left Giglio. And then our middle-school years, which placed an enormous distance between boys and girls, did the rest.

But towards the end of the summer when we were sixteen, we discovered that we were a boy and girl that had known and liked each other since we were little, and the beautiful experiences that we had shared together weren't over yet.

Caterina and I had spent all of August with Vittorio in Giglio. We hung out with the same group, with a propensity for Luigi's friends, whom he had brought from Rome. With the Gigliesi it had become difficult to find common ground. We had become girls from the mainland. Pietro was always wild, and this did not change while he was growing up. He did the same things he did as a child, just a bit more seriously: fishing and driving boats. He was also able to earn some money during the summer by leading tourists on diving tours and selling the fish he caught to restaurants. Girls liked him a lot, because he was handsome, always tan, and not afraid of anything. But I didn't. The way he spoke bothered me, the fact that he knew nothing about music, he never read, and the thoughts I had in my head never had anything in common with his. Often, we didn't know what to say when we were together. We found a small shared interest in his little sister Lucia. She was born by surprise eleven years after him. She was a sweet girl with dark braids and bright and mysterious clear eyes, a type of yellow granite, sparkling with curiosity. During the summer, their parents left her with Pietro while they worked so he took her with him, and we kept her with us. Lucia had a soft spot for me.

She would look for me, she often sat next to me, she wanted me to redo her braids or to put sunscreen on her. One morning towards the end of summer, I went to the sea early to enjoy the last days there and found Lucia waiting for Pietro on the rocks while he was diving. Every so often he would come up for air, with the skeleton of a sea urchin or a starfish for her. In the distance, we saw him reemerge with a tiny octopus that was clinging onto his hands. He called Lucia to show her its hideout. We joined him by jumping from the rocks. The octopus detached itself, stretched itself, wrapped around a stone, quickly changed color, becoming violet, then grey, and lit up white like a lamp. It pushed itself off with its tentacles and returned to its hideout. Lucia was ready to cry, "Why did you let it go?"

"Be good," Pietro told her. "Now I'll show you a game." He got out of the water and moved quickly between the rocks. He captured a small crab. He took out a thin twine from the knapsack he always had with him and tied the crab with it by a claw. Then he threw it in front of the octopus' hideout. Shortly after, the animal came out, grabbed the crab, changed color, wrapped back onto itself, and went back in. Lucia watched in awe.

"If you feed it every day, you could come and play with it."

"It doesn't swim away?"

"No, this is its home. If you put on the mask, I'll show you. The octopus arranges its hole, it puts pebbles and shells in front of the door. It recognizes its home. And you can make the octopus yours."

"Yes, it's mine, it's mine." He gave her the twine and dove back into the water, so I tried the trick a few times to make it come out, but it wasn't interested in what we had to offer. I convinced Lucia that it wasn't hungry anymore and had fallen asleep in the hole. I watched Pietro's shiny body in the distance. I thought of Colapesce, who, if he existed, would have looked like Pietro.

Before joining the group again, as we jumped off the rocks behind Lucia, Pietro told me, "Tomorrow I will take you on my boat, we'll go with the small one. Be at the lighthouse cafe at ten." The next morning, we met, and I thought Lucia would come too, but it was just me and him alone. I followed him without asking for an explanation.

We cast off and didn't say anything until the anchor touched the sandy bottom of the cove and, turning his dark and muscular back to me while tying the knot, he said, "I don't like the way you've treated me this summer."

"Look who's talking. And how have you treated me?"

"Look Tere, don't piss me off. You came here because you want to ease your conscience on the last day of summer and now you're accusing me. The few moments that you paid attention to me, you did it to shit on me with your high-school friends and those Chateaubriand people that you like so much. Am I a vulgar ignoramus, a shit boatman who's not on your level? It's okay if I am, but don't you get pissed off because I treat you badly. Go get on their speedboats and leave me alone."

I gave him an astonished look.

"Pietro, you're the one who's making this a big deal. I don't understand why you're jealous—we haven't been close this summer. I'll leave you here in peace. You were the one that asked me to come here with you. We're not in elementary school anymore, we've grown up now and each of us has gone down our own path. *Sticazzi*, who gives a fuck, right?"

"Oh God, you speak Roman dialect now. I can't stand you."

"Why did you ask me to come here? Go fuck yourself."

He didn't respond and dove into the sea. I dove in too and swam to the rocks on the other side of the cove, determined not to go back with him, I would rather have hitched a ride. He got back on the boat and ignored my absence. He dove back in with a mask and a knife, and in half an hour he had pulled up a bunch of sea urchins. He placed them on the bow and pulled up the anchor. I knew that he would leave, and I didn't pay any attention to him, lying down on my rock.

Instead, he came over, put the boat in neutral, and said, "Come on, let's go eat them at Fenaio."

I dove in and got back onto the boat. It was empty at Fenaio's cove. From afar, we were two dark spots on a blue and gold background. Pietro cut open the sea urchins and with the tiny spoon from his pocket knife started to scoop out the pulp, which he passed to me after eating some himself. When we finished, I laid down on the bow without saying a word. Pietro laid down next to me and put a hand on my neck. He squeezed a bit and said, "Damn you," through clenched teeth. I opened my eyes and I pulled myself up to fall over him. His body was very hot. He held me. He brought his lips close to mine and gave me a kiss. A kiss that felt like a magical fluid, that slowly made me fall under its spell.

I let him do it, with every touch I felt a pressure from inside that surfaced onto my skin. His hands, his lips had a magnetic force. We ended up making love, there on the boat, under the sun. We were in a place that was out in the open, overexposed and perhaps unfit for the circumstance, which normally called for twilight, when it came to our nudity, my very pale breasts, Pietro's erection, which I couldn't manage to look at, my lowered eyelid under which I saw red, and his heart, which I felt beating hard. That beginning, so warm and illuminated, had its own future. It was my first time, but not his. He was inside me very briefly. It hurt me, also because of the salt we had all over us, and everything burned inside and out. There was a second time. At a certain point, while Pietro was on top of me, I grabbed a small sea urchin and I stuck it into his back, while I held him tight. He yelled and bit my lip. Then he sucked it, and from there began to trace my body with his tongue, following its edges along every curve, and from the care that he put into that exploratory journey, it was clear to me that he had been in love with me for a long time. And I discovered many things with him, most of all the power of his body on mine and mine on his, and it was a spectacular thing, that moon landing in the middle of the sea. I went back home like an astronaut returning from a mission, with a look of surprise, an unsteady gait, and with Pietro's flag planted onto my heart, waving without gravity.

Pietro too was about to move to Porto Santo Stefano, because he had signed up for the nautical institute after having repeated the eighth grade. After that last day in Giglio, we exchanged the phone numbers for our homes on the mainland, which were also quite close, but we never called each other. School began, without notice, and as long as the weather was nice, Pietro would occasionally come to pick me up on his scooter outside of school in Orbetello and we did the *salino*, as they called it around there. We skipped school to go to some deserted beach in Monte Argentario, between the dunes of the Feniglia, to make love, like two wild animals, always a bit angry with each other, pleased with the bruises that we got from the pleasure of rolling our bony sixteen-year-old bodies over those pebbles smoothed down by years of waves. We were an age when we didn't get tired or really hurt. There wasn't much romance, but that was our way of coming together. When winter came and I began to study seriously, I skipped those adventures a couple of times and then Pietro stopped passing by to try to pick me up in the mornings. I called him, before Christmas break, to tell him that I would be going to visit him the next Sunday, when his mother was away in Giglio. I missed him. And when we saw each other again, such a passion took us over that we forgot about our tacit pact of anger. During that Christmas break, we behaved like a real couple. Gifts and afternoons together, hand in hand, long kisses, and a romance that didn't belong to us. Then we resumed pretending to not love each other.

Pietro was too ignorant for me. And I couldn't come to terms with his resistance to school. I was a nerd and curious about everything. I would often interrogate him. "What did you learn this year in school?" "To tie knots," he would respond. "Where will you go after graduation?" I would ask him, knowing that he would join a crew and that he had no intention of going to college. But he didn't react, he didn't feel the need to prove anything. I would speak to him and it was as if, between the lines, I was saying, "I'm a heavyweight, you're a lightweight, we can't fight in the same ring." He stayed silent and it was as if he responded, "But Teresa, we're not boxing, we're dancing."

We broke up every summer. And without hesitation he took advantage of the fascination he exerted over foreigners. I would leave him to do as he pleased. Jealousy and a mutual pseudo-indifference masquerading as freedom were part of our way of being together, like a subtle perversion. Sometimes we met in secret, behind the backs of our respective summer partners; it was a bond that we wanted to pass off to both ourselves and others as half farce, a superficial relationship without substance, but in reality it lasted a long time, much longer than our expectations. Even when I moved to Milan to study, everyone knew him as my boyfriend of three years already, and he would remain that, on and off, for at least another three.

Then he fell in love with one of those foreigners. And she got pregnant, so they got married, started a family, and so it was that at twenty-nine years old he had a four-year-old son and a beautiful Irish wife with red hair, who from afar looked like Caterina, which did not seem to me like just a coincidence.

19.

Anyway, Pietro was water under the bridge. But it would be hard for me to run into him, those kisses on the cheek to say

hello that we weren't able to give each other, keeping our distance, the meaningless small talk under which we needed to
pretend to bury the intimacy that brought us together, the look
on his face that said, "That's how it goes." I preferred to avoid
him. So, getting off the ferry, I put on my sunglasses and
walked past him and his son without catching their eyes.

I walked home, holding my carry-on because the wheels
made an unbearable noise, amplified by the hollowness of the
port. I didn't see anyone except for a scraggly cat that came
towards me as I was catching my breath after the first climb. It
followed me until I got to the door, rubbing up against my leg
while I looked for the key, which was in its usual hiding spot
under the overturned plant dish.

I went inside and opened all the windows. I hoped that
the mistral would carry away the stench of an unopened
house with a whirlwind through the rooms. Instead, the windows began to rattle, and the doors shut with a bang. Then I
secured the shutters and locked the windows, and the humid-
ity held me; it was perhaps part of the house, like in vacation
homes by the beach. But this was never a vacation home. My
father still lived here; it was a single man's home. It was
cleaned by a maid who didn't know where to put his stuff.

During the years we all lived there, there was always a
mixed smell of fresh paint, doll hair, and meals cooked with
patience. An irreproducible smell, which was still there if you
searched for it well, but back then there had been no traces of
the brackish mold that now covered everything. And what had
happened to all those people who used to come through our
home, the infinite dinners, Nonna who threw the sheet of
dough on the round table to make tagliatelle? The table was
still there, a few folding chairs too. But it was all deserted.

Alice had lived there for barely a year after we left, then she
left too. For a long time, the smell of her Aromatics Elixir
lingered in the rooms, but eventually that vanished as well.

Dad never talked about it anymore, and he didn't seem particularly hurt by her leaving either. He let her leave with the same sense of inevitability with which he had allowed her long legs to intrude on his family. At that point he had strung together a series of temporary girlfriends that he passed off as friends and when we visited, he would ask them to sleep somewhere else so he wouldn't have to explain them. But his drawers remained full of photos of Alice, hundreds of photos in black and white, tons of portraits, in particular of her body, taken with a macro lens.

I was going to look for him at the hotel or at the bar. He still didn't have a cell phone. I put my suitcase and coat in the room and then stopped to look at his things: his few clothes, very colorful and stylish, the closet with all the mismatched linen, the book that he had on the nightstand, the debut of a Jewish American author with whom he shared a certain curiosity towards the other sex, the audiocassettes of Lucio Dalla and jazz classics. The tenderness of his safe choices, of someone who did not keep up with the latest fads. I went down to the kitchen to look for something to eat. There was only pasta, toast, and a jar of marmalade covered in mold. I made myself a coffee with mineral water, scratched off some sugar from its congealed single block, mixed it in the plastic espresso cup from a set for a boat and took it out onto the terrace. I let the wind smoke three cigarettes while waiting for the sunset. The cat was still there and came to sit close to me. It purred while I sneezed. About a year ago, I had found out I had become allergic. Pollution, the doctors said. I kept it close to me anyway—my eyes itched, even though I didn't touch it, but I liked feeling the slight pressure from its thin and fluffy body and the running motor of its bliss on my leg. Watching the light from the lighthouse become more and more intense against the dark background, a shiver ran through me that freed me from my immobility. I couldn't bear that open horizon with the first stars for long. My city views were polluted. They gave me limits. They were bearable. This open sky by the sea was not.

I headed towards the San Lorenzo hotel. The Antonionis, the family that helped my dad manage the hotel after my mom left, were expecting me for dinner; my father had told them I was coming.

Vittorio arrived with a twenty-pound bottle of oil, which he deposited with a sharp blow on the counter before coming to hug me, panting.

"It's so great that you came, Tere." He was happy like always to see me, but something was off, he was older and thinner.

"Oh, yeah, I thought I'd come surprise you by myself. Are you doing okay?"

"Yes, everything's fine. I'm always tired, I don't know, I don't feel very in shape. I'm getting old."

"It's because you live like you're still thirty. You challenge yourself. But you look thinner. Do you ever get yourself checked out?"

"No."

"You should."

He immediately dropped the subject. They had prepared linguine with lobster and baked turbot for me, and it didn't seem real because the windows were open, and I ate fish with the sounds of undertow in the background. It was only us. They made me talk about Rome and I spoke with false enthusiasm about my job, how rewarding it was, and how many experiences I had, including at an international level. I left out that I was suffering from gastritis, as well as allergies that I'd never had previously. That in reality, I'd only taken one trip abroad that lasted two days. And that I was nauseous every morning before going to the office. And above all, I had earned less in one year than Edo the boatman does at the end of the season. We talked about the present and the future, first using clichés, and then, as the rust-colored flask of Ansonaco gradually emptied, we started pontificating, and finally, when there was no more and our sentences came out suspended in subordinate clauses that struggled to meet one another, we began to yawn shamelessly. I told Dad that it was time for us to go. We took a flashlight and headed towards home. Along the way we didn't say a word. It seemed that it was too much effort for him to climb the stairs and also talk. At a certain point, when we had almost gotten all the way up the one hundred steps that separated us from the door, he stopped. He took a breath.

"What's wrong? Why did you stop?"

"Nothing, I wanted to look at the stars."

In fact, there was a sky that only existed there. A sky completely turned off and pitch-black, with the stars polished by the north wind. That was the roof of my home. I felt an emotion surge that I forced myself to control. I placed my arm around my father and told him to come in, that it was cold out. He asked if I wanted to sleep in his room. I knew it would make him happy, but I was twenty-nine years old and I couldn't sleep next to someone that snored.

The next morning, he went out early and left me to sleep. I woke up around ten, with the only noise coming from the obsessive triplets of turtledoves on our pine tree. I went down to have breakfast at the cafe. There was only one open. Besides me, there were three other customers. By the way they were dressed, they looked like bricklayers. Poles or Romanians. The youngest-looking one was missing two front teeth. They all ordered lattes. The barista, without batting an eye, poured three glasses of neat Campari with sambuca. Well, it was true what people said, that these days, during the winter, the only things going around were the wild sheep, alcohol, and hard drugs. I ordered a cappuccino. And for a split second I thought I saw the barista go towards the bottle of Fernet. I stayed there for a while. There weren't any newspapers, they hadn't arrived yet, so I began reading a statement for hunters about the previous hunting season. I left the bar with the same furtive haste with which I had entered, opening the door with my shoulder as to not take my hands out of my pockets. I felt cold. I tucked my head into my coat and looked up. In front of me was a stretch of sea that seemed to end everything on the darker line that divided the sky from the earth, the horizon without an after. That was enough to believe in God.

I breathed heavily in the wind. I headed slowly towards the hotel. I was walking along the deserted port, hunched over to protect myself from the wind, watching the overturned boats on the shore, when I heard someone call me. I turned but the street was empty. "Hey, I'm over here." The voice came from the other side. It was Pietro on the roof of the house above the real-estate agency office, with a polyester jumpsuit on and a Juventus striped wool cap. "I'm fixing Beppina's antenna, this wind disconnected it." I smiled at him and he realized that he hadn't greeted me, as if we had just recently seen each other. He yelled, "How's it going? I knew you were here—yesterday you pretended not to see me when you got off the ferry."

He joined me on the ground.

"I came on a solo trip," I responded and, luckily, I didn't think to add that phrase about unplugging. "And you?"

"I'm almost always here now. I go offshore as little as possible. Callum's in kindergarten. Deirdre works with the Internet."

"Callum . . . Deirdre. What kind of fucking names are those?"

"Deirdre is Irish."

"Yeah, but Callum is from Giglio . . ."

"It's his grandfather's name."

"Oh, of course."

"What about you? Do you have a boyfriend?"

"No. Well, I'm seeing someone, but . . . you know me and relationships, couples, long stories. So, mind your fucking business," I said laughing. He began to laugh too and without warning, he hugged me. I was captive between his shoulders long enough for the gesture to lose its innocence. He said in my ear, "Teresa . . ."

I interrupted him and wriggled out.

"My father told me that in about a month or so you guys are going to compete in a regatta, right?"

"Yeah, we're competing in the Vele d'Argento in April. With Pistelli's vintage boat, the dentist from Orbetello. After this year it won't be called that anymore. They've renamed it Argentario 'Sailing Week,' to make it sound international."

"Nice. You'll have fun, right?"

"With Vittorio? Of course."

"Listen, I'm going to go meet up with him, I'm here to spend time with him. Bye Pietro, take care."

"Bye beautiful."

Dad was behind the front desk yelling at the computer. I helped him manage the customers' documents. I reminded him of how, when Caterina was little, they had taken advantage of her exceptional memory to remember the birthdays of all the regulars so they could wish them a happy birthday. She would bring up a birthday every day more or less—she got used to it and had catalogued almost everyone. I pointed out to my father that it was a free, cutting-edge strategy for customer care.

"I don't know what that means but it sounds nice," he said to me.

"You realized early on that making the customers feel taken care of, letting them know that you'll never forget about them, makes them think of you when it's time for them to choose who to go to again. It's marketing."

"Great, and we spent all that money to send you to Bocconi

University so you could learn things we already knew on our own?"

"Unfortunately, yes. A waste of money! It would've been better if you had bought a sailboat."

"Hey, you laugh, but I think that might be true."

I suggested that we take a walk to Capel Rosso and then have lunch at the Castello. He agreed to have lunch, but about the walk he suggested we go until the red pier. That to walk the remaining half a mile would take us an hour, what with having to greet and be polite to everyone we'd come across. Once we were alone on the pier, we sat with our faces towards the sun on the step at the foot of the lighthouse and brought up the topic that always united us: the dislike we had for Caterina's man. We aired out our rosary prayers: that she would liberate herself from that narcissistic artist, that she would rebel against his insistence that they be together with absolutely no kids, that she would end this human sacrifice, and that the end of her love would lead her to see with her own eyes, always the most observant of all, who this Hervé really was.

Then he suddenly asked me, "And what about you?"

"Me, nothing, Dad. I mean, not nothing nothing, I'm not that much of a loser. But I haven't found the one yet."

"It's not that you found him and let him go? I know you're a bit like me, you always understand things after the fact, when it's already too late."

"Dad, I don't know what you're referring to, but you're wrong. Too late for what? I'm twenty-nine years old. Keep your sentimentalism for your own self-awareness, thanks."

I got up and walked away. He caught up with me and we took the car to go to the Castello. That day and the next morning went by very slowly. I read, he did too, we ate, went on walks, talked about politics, and when I waved to him from the ferry my heart hurt to see him like that, a bit hunched over in his raincoat that looked like it was a size too big, his hair thinning, a red dot of loneliness on the rock-colored background.

20.

That was the last time. And for the rest of my life, I was grateful to have responded to that instinct, to the telegram from Caterina, that had brought me home to see him, during that false spring.

About a month later, during the Vele d'Argento regatta, Vittorio had a heart attack on the boat.

Pietro told me that he was straightening the jib after a warmup when he suddenly stopped, letting go of the top to free one arm and to bring the other to his chest. The whole crew stopped while the loose sail began to flutter. Not understanding what was going on, the owner of the boat swore because the maneuver wasn't working and the boom had come down on the leeward side, threatening to hit his head. It seems it all happened very fast. Once they realized that my dad had collapsed at the helm, they let go of the sails, started the engine, sounded an alarm, radioed the harbormaster, who was on a boat nearby, while someone attempted an awkward cardiac massage. And when a patrol boat from the Guardia di Finanza that was close by came and took him away, at most ten minutes had passed. Ten minutes at sea aren't ten minutes on land. In any case, from there to the port, from the port to the ambulance, and from Porto Santo Stefano to the hospital in Orbetello, on a Sunday in April on which everyone had reopened their houses by the sea and the roads were crowded, enough time had passed to kill Dad.

Mom was the first to know and arrived at the hospital only after nothing could be done. But Pietro was the one to tell me. I was at the beach with my girlfriends in Ostia. There was a joy that would soon become guilt on that spring day, young and beautiful girls wearing sleeveless dresses and sunglasses, chatting and laughing at nothing, helped by the prosecco and the ridiculous guys that paraded before them, and when my phone rang and I saw Pietro's number, I immediately said to Federica and Anna, "Huh, it's my ex-boyfriend from Giglio; who knows what he wants, he'll probably tell me that he's still in love with me." And when I answered, I don't even remember what he said, but in my mind, I have a clear memory in the third person, as if I had left my body: I watched this girl jump up from the table, run on the beach, and scream, "What? What did you say? When? How? Where is he now?" and then suddenly put her phone in her bag and grab onto a fence, gag a couple of times, though nothing really came out except for a strangled sound which gave way to a long, low sob, and then I saw her group of three girlfriends bring their hands to their mouths and hug her, and then the phone came out of the bag again and the girl with straight hair waved her hand and wiped her cheeks, and from there, from her mother's voice onwards, the scene returned to the first person and it became a very long car ride along the Aurelia highway, a drive that she'd done a thousand times before, but this time it was heavy and never-ending. And the whole way, alongside my friend Anna who came with me, my thoughts about Vittorio weren't a list of good memories, like the ones you have once someone has passed. Instead, it was a series of regrets, mistakes, things said badly or not at all, and the feeling that prevailed was the pain of an absence that in some ways had always been there and that I had never been able to fill. The frustration of never being able to obey him, and to have lost him without ever having done so. Poor Daddy, poor Daddy, I never agreed with him. Neither I nor my sister. His wife, never. Maybe not even his own mother. He was a man who died without ever once being right.

It's strange to say, since there were two hundred people at

the funeral, so many that they didn't even all fit in the church, but for me it was a mourning that only belonged to us, me and Caterina.

Not even our own mother, who was the first to rush to the hospital, the first to identify him, to dress him well, to pick out the coffin, to pay for the funeral, was entitled to suffer as much as Caterina and I, in my opinion. Or as much as I was, really, because it was clear that if there were a special place in his damaged heart, I occupied it, more than anyone else. More than Caterina, more than Mom, more than all his sailing friends, his fishing friends, his hunting friends, his cantina friends, the butcher, the tobacco-shop owner, the baker, the boatman, the barista, the newspaper man, the landlord, the hairdresser, the teacher, the plumber, and the municipal employees combined. More than all of his lovers who showed up to the funeral crying and dressed all in black, Alice included. Alice, who came to hug me, and I let her, once more, and I heard, once more, the umpteenth version of, "He wouldn't have wanted to die any other way, there couldn't have been a better way. He didn't even realize what was happening. He went away just like that, instantaneously, at sea, while having fun, while doing what he loved. He wouldn't have wanted anything else," and me not responding with, "Go fuck yourself Alice. Maybe if you had stayed with him you could've realized that he wasn't okay. Maybe if you hadn't abandoned him you could've helped him take care of himself and he wouldn't have died of a broken heart. You shitty doctor. That's what he would've wanted at fifty-nine—my ass. No, he would've still wanted other things, so many, like living to see the new millennium, maybe grandchildren, some more sun, wind, and lots of the sea until old age. Who told you that this was what he wanted, asshole?" And instead, I said, "I know, I know," and I returned her hug, within which, just as I had when I was a kid, I felt her irresistible softness. I loved everyone in that moment.

Then I became afflicted with a type of logorrhea. I told everyone that a few weeks before, I had felt a hunch that I should go see him, that I took time off to visit him in Giglio. I almost knew it. That, in fact, I had seen he wasn't well. That he was fatigued while climbing the stairs, that I could've, that we should've helped. I repeated it to everyone and invariably the response was, "In bad health, it's better this way. Think about a chronic illness. He wouldn't have been able to handle it." As if getting rid of this thought could somehow alleviate the pain of his absence. And as much I talked, welcomed, and responded to everyone, my sister remained apart, silent, on the edge of muteness. She would shake hands with whomever approached her, and in her elegant clothes she withdrew herself without leaving room for anything more than a condolence, standing guard over mother Elena, even more on the sidelines than her, flanked on the other side by Nonnalina. I saved them from the Overkills, who had come from Rome, Desi wearing a low-cut satin dress and desperate diva sunglasses, and Sergio who cried like a baby, repeating, "I can't believe it, he was the liveliest man in the world." I nodded, holding his hand, dragging him far away from my mother.

We buried him in the port's cemetery, the one on the way to the Cannelle beach, where, if it wasn't for the seawall that blocks the view, it would be the most beautiful place in the world to rest in peace, in front of a stretch of the sea, with the sunrise on the island of Giannutri to make you think you're already in heaven. We threw dirt on the coffin, waited for the long work of the gravediggers to be done, which began with them filling in the hole, then arranging the bricks and fresh concrete, and I kept my jaw shut because they were incredibly slow and indifferent, as if they were repairing a road or some wall but it was my father there, goddammit, they needed to hurry up, they needed to do the job like it should be done. I wanted that moment to be over, I wanted to go home, I wanted to return to Rome to not find parking, I wanted to return to work, to work like a dog on my stupid market research, on toothpaste benchmarking, I wanted to be in Caterina's beautiful apartment in Paris talking poorly about him, I wanted to call him around seven-thirty in the evening because I knew I would catch him at home getting ready to go out to dinner with someone, I wanted to buy him his favorite lavender perfume and talk about books, I wanted to be six years old and go on the boat with him, to be eight years old and receive effusive compliments because I had made coffee using the Moka pot and there wasn't a better cup in the world than mine, I wanted the restaurant to reserve the best table for us, because in his little world, he had the ability to be loved by everyone, I wanted everyone to go away and leave me alone with that pain which was mine alone and I didn't want to share it with anyone else, because no man had ever loved me like he did, never, never, never. In the vortex of all that useless wanting that smeared together alongside the mortar, I found myself on my knees crying with both hands on the fresh cement to stamp them forever into it and Pietro pulling me up and me evading him, because it wasn't his hug that I wanted. Because no matter how much he tried to give me comfort, how many times he dried my tears with his enormous hands, I could not avoid the thought that he had always been there when I was missing something important. Pietro was there to say goodbye when I left Giglio, he had found my dead dog, run over on the side of the road; Pietro when I lost my virginity, Pietro when my father died. And I hated him for it.

We got home very late. It was just us women. It was a moment when suddenly, between those walls where arguments had resounded, laughter or the slamming of doors, there fell an unusual peace, when we talked in low voices, asking for things with pleases and thank yous. It was the first time in eighteen years that we were all there together. Nonnalina was upset about the mess, most of all in the kitchen, shook her head and tidied up, the only way for her to fill up her time being small gestures of care and cleaning. No one was hungry, but she found it immoral to not prepare something and she managed to whip up a meal that we devoured.

We were exhausted. Mom didn't want to sleep in her old bed, so she and Nonna took the bedroom that I used to share with my sister. Caterina and I were stuck with the queen bed, whose sheet we changed, but still we weren't able to get rid of Dad's scent.

Caterina was incredibly quiet; before and after dinner I saw her furiously typing messages on her phone with her thumbs and her expression becoming more unsettled. Ever since she was a kid, she would cry easily when she was angry, but sadness terrified her, and I didn't see her shed a tear. We went to bed hoping the fatigue would take care of the rest, but that was obviously wishful thinking. Maybe we just needed to lie there in the dark, under the covers, in the fetal position to simulate that reassuring moment, full of the promises of life before life had begun. Cate and I, her behind and me in front, hugging like twins in the womb, spent the whole night like that, only falling asleep once we could hear the fishing boats leaving the port, after having talked about everything, about life and men, because she, on the same day that we buried our dad, whom she had considered to be a selfish man who was incapable of unconditional love, had left Hervé, "Another man," she said, "made in the exact same way, who was incapable of doing something just for me, wouldn't even come with me to my father's funeral. I never asked him for anything, I never interfered with his work, I even helped it. It's the first thing, the only thing that I've asked him to do with me, for me, and he told me he couldn't."

I supported her. I could never stand Hervé. I couldn't

stand anyone that stole her love away from me and even less someone that made her suffer. I hated that the strength, the independence that Caterina had always shown, had been crushed by a relationship that dominated her. I feared that the attraction that she felt for Hervé was because they shared similar souls: that was the side of Caterina that I always had trouble putting up with, her need to excel, to be a part of important circles, to reject our islander attitude for the useless rich-and-famous bourgeois, her snobbery, even towards me, that I hated. When Hervé was around, I wasn't able to love Caterina. I couldn't recognize her in that couple, nor could I separate her out, see her as an individual, as still being her, as someone different from that chronically narcissistic sculptor.

I didn't have the courage to tell her all of this. I constrained myself to supporting her, helping her muster up the strength, agreeing with her complaints, and telling her that it would do her good to liberate herself from him.

The next morning, Mom told us we needed to get to work on the closet, to fill up bags with Vittorio's clothes and shoes to take them to the Red Cross, to throw away what could be thrown out, and to organize the linens and towels. They entrusted me with the worst part, possibly as retaliation for being his favorite. I had to go through his drawers and touch every pair of faded underwear, every undershirt, the sad pajamas, whose worn-out patterns and the creases that formed when he wore them I knew from memory. An arrow pierced my heart.

I forced myself to fill up my black bag, even if with every piece of clothing I had the temptation to say, I'll keep this, I'll wear it to bed. In the back of the underwear drawer, I found a box without a lid that had some valuables.

In the box were Grandpa's gold watch, a checkbook, a money order, an envelope with 200,000 lire, a small box with a pound of gold packed with wadding, a black and white photo of Caterina and I laughing with Irma on the back of a Piaggio Ape, and a closed envelope with "For the babies" written on it, in his handwriting, unmistakable, crowded, and shaky. To save time, he would always call us "the babies" ever since we were little. "I'm going to see the babies." "The babies are here," he would say to his friends, who would make fun of him because over time we became little girls, then young women, and finally women.

I opened the envelope. It didn't even cross my mind for a second that I should wait for my sister.

> *Dear Babies,*
> *who are now women, beautiful, intelligent, and strong, if you're reading this, it's probably because I'm no longer there. My heart isn't working well, but I'm unable to live like someone who's sick, so I preferred to not tell you anything and wait for the moment to arrive, continuing to do the things I'm capable of, the things that I'm used to. Retirement, rest, being careful, aren't for me. Apparently it's happened now, and I ask you both to forgive me if I didn't leave you with enough time to tell me everything you'd want to tell me before I go. But don't worry, I knew everything that was important to know and you have nothing to blame yourselves for, the two of you were amazing daughters. And everything that you might have wanted to blame me for, over the years, I've already blamed myself for. I don't have much to leave you, except for this house where we had many good times. I don't have any advice to give, because you already know what's best for you. Seek your happiness any way that you can and don't let anyone force you into taking a different path than the one you want to get there.*
> *I know you're not interested, but I would like the hotel to stay in the family. I would also like very much, but didn't dare ask because I know that any question I ask her directly will*

only receive a "No" in response, that your mother, as the only person I blindly trust, manage the hotel. Perhaps you both have also understood that our marriage was a big misunderstanding from the beginning. We were not made for each other and neither of us had a knack for the life of a couple. But this does not mean that we did not love each other and that at the end of the day, if I think back to all the things I've done in my life, the single most beautiful one, the thing that I am truly proud of and that has made me a lucky man, is what I made with her: the two of you. And for how you have grown up, even if for the most part I've been left out of this process, I have nothing but gratitude towards her. So I'm asking you now for one more favor: try to convince her. Perhaps it wouldn't be so bad for her, as a capable and organized person, to think about returning here in her old age and occupying herself with the grandkids who will come to visit, saving them a nice corner spot in the sun in front of the sea. I'll watch her from the other side, with a bit of jealousy. In my will I've left San Lorenzo to her, but if you don't convince her, she'll probably sell it. Tell her that I've always loved her, because it's been so long since I've talked to her, and it's been just as long since she doesn't trust me, so I can't tell her if not through you. I'm sure you two will understand. Goodbye my babies, I love you both very much,

Daddy
11/12/1997

The letter had been written a year and a half before that moment. I called Caterina over and made her read it. She shook her head and finally cried. She cried like someone who had been holding it back, streams of tears wetting her cheeks, chin, and neck. Then she said to me, "Don't even think about actually trying to convince Mom."

When we showed Elena, she cried too, then folded up the

sheet three times and put it in her pocket. I didn't dare to tell her that the letter wasn't hers.

The first to speak was Caterina: "He's a smartass even when he's dead. He guilt-trips Mom and assumes we'll convince her to uproot her life and take over the fucking hotel, which is drowning in debt."

Mom snapped: "Caterina, please! We buried him yesterday: can you, at least for a day, try to have respect for your father, the bit of posthumous respect everyone deserves?"

"Oh God. You seem as though you're talking about a stranger! Saying things about him, about how he was, doesn't change how much I loved him. The truth isn't a lack of respect, but I've clashed with the both of you my whole life on this topic. Our dad was a wise guy. He never stopped being one."

"Of course the hotel is in debt, I know it. And it's not clear that even selling or leasing it would be enough to settle those debts. We need to see the accounts. Either way, I won't be coming back to Giglio. Don't even try talking me into it. My job and my life are somewhere else," Mom said, touching the pocket where she kept the letter.

Two months later she was at the reception desk with her glasses on her nose learning from Irene Antonioni how to use the computer program that managed the reservations. I didn't do anything to convince her, and Caterina was completely opposed: "Giglio is a prison, don't you remember, Mom?" She was one to talk, since in the meantime she had gotten back together with Hervé.

Mom uncovered the debt, decided angrily that it could be resolved with a bit of hard work, paying attention to costs, and without liquidating everything. She did it for us. For our futures, because we shouldn't take on our father's debt. Because there was still something there. But we never asked her to. Caterina tried to advise her, but there's nothing harder for a child than to assist in the voluntary sacrifice of a parent who then says, "I did it for you."

That "I did it for you" made me cancel a trip to India that I'd planned with Federica and Anna, to lend a hand at the hotel. It was out of the question that Caterina would come. She had work and a short vacation on the French Riviera with some artist friends of Hervé's.

I settled in, and deep down I didn't feel very sad about what I'd given up. I found myself like my dad, loyal to my sea. Loyal to the pain of his loss and completely devoid of initiative. All it took was a nod from Elena and there I was, in Giglio for the thirtieth summer, mourning in the sad hotel without Vittorio, immersed in the fake hospitality sprinkled with hatred of the Gigliesi, who couldn't wait for everyone to leave, visiting my former classmates perfunctorily and without passion, who by now had grown children and wore heels that were too tall, from whose heights they looked down at me, unleashing all the complexed haughtiness of the islanders.

There were also consolations, after having collected the clean sheets from the laundry, calling all the suppliers for the orders, and verifying the check-out payments: the hot granite on which I went to lie down, the dives, and long swims in the sea in front of San Lorenzo; but nothing was the same. Everything there reminded me of a different version from my childhood, taller, more majestic, more magical.

21.

Then came the last week of August. The prelude before the end of summer vacation, during which life in Giglio had always reserved unexpected discoveries for me, full of growth. The tests at the end of summer, those that said listen up, this hot and lazy time of yours is soon to expire, do something memorable now.

An odd-numbered group had arrived at the San Lorenzo, a couple plus one. They were from Milan: a brother, a sister, and her husband. They were all over forty and the couple was passionate about diving. The man on his own wasn't. While he waited for the others to return after six hours with their wetsuits dripping, which he glanced at with disgust, he read.

He would spend his mornings under the breakfast veranda, with the waiters who would clear and then set the tables for the evening, without moving. During the cooler hours he'd lie down on the rocks. Sometimes he would go up to his room, but for the entirety of the first and second day, he practically didn't move from the perimeter of the hotel, always with a book in hand. He was tall, had a beard and glasses with frames that would soon become too fashionable. He walked with a limp and, despite the heat, always wore long pants and closed-toe shoes. I would pass in front of him to spy on the backs of the books, every day a different one, all American literature. One morning I found the courage to ask if I could drink my coffee at his table, since everyone else had left and that was the best spot, with the breeze that came from the sea. He smiled and said, "Of course," and I noticed that he looked at my breasts before placing the open book down on the table. It was *Girl with Curious Hair*. We talked for a while. His name was Enrico, he was a mathematics professor and confessed that this was his dream the whole summer, to find himself in front of the sea and with nothing to do except read the books that he had bought and didn't have time to open. I nodded and said that I also liked American literature and that I also didn't have much time to read. He looked at me, perplexed. He had very light blue eyes with a darker blue around the edges, a challenge for an awe-prone person like me. "But don't you have the entire winter . . ."

"With shit all to do?" I chuckled. "No, I work in Rome. I'm just here to give my mom a hand. I studied economics at Bocconi; I work in marketing."

"Really, then you've lived in Milan?"

"Yes. But I'll leave you to your book now. Otherwise, I'll ruin your vacation."

How strategic I had been to get up at that point.

"As soon as you feel a bite, give it a strong pull, and then let the line go a little slack." Pietro's fishing lessons came in handy on many occasions.

He smiled and nodded; I could feel that he watched me as I walked away.

Now I just needed to reel him in little by little. I couldn't wait for that evening.

It was just past ten and I was in the sitting room in the lobby, alone. During the summer nobody stayed in the lobby: everyone preferred to go out on the veranda or to walk on the rocks. I saw the group of three returning from dinner, laughing loudly, and I greeted them with a nod.

Noticing me, Enrico pulled himself up more rigidly on the crutch that helped him walk. He stopped, said goodnight to the other two, then came and sat next to me.

We sat there for more than two hours. I learned that he was forty-one and an associate professor of mathematics at the University of Milan. He described himself as a "probability researcher." He talked to me a bit about his work and his studies on stochastic processes that had been published in international journals, in particular his articles on the applications of Markov chains. He also tried to explain what it was about in basic terms and I think I used every fiber of my brain to understand what he was saying. The perception of my ignorance made me feel defeated. Defeated and attracted. Because nothing made me more curious than what I didn't know. I wasn't able to extract any information about Enrico's love life. All I knew was that he traveled often. Then it was my turn. I didn't like talking about myself very much. I'd rather know everything about him. But since he wouldn't open up about himself, I did so, telling him a bit about my business.

I told him about my relationship with Milan, my arrival there, the initial sense of loss. I told him about the attempts to shake off the remnants of a provincialism so ingrained that the word provincialism wasn't enough to describe it, it was so much more, it was an islander attitude, an abyss of peripherality. I told him about my sister in Paris, the death of my father, and my job in Rome. I tried to make a good impression; I talked too much.

When it was his turn, I waited for him to say something about his limp, but he didn't mention it, and I sensed it was something more serious and painful than an accident, and which he didn't want to talk about. At a certain point he nudged my arm and proposed that we go outside to smoke. It was almost midnight. I wanted us to climb up the tall rock because it was one of my favorite spots to smoke, but for ease I took him to the port, where there was a bench in front of the fishing boats. I asked if he could roll me a cigarette and after placing my lips on the paper he had just licked, I felt that the beautiful part was about to begin: the waiting period before real contact.

Deirdre and Lucia passed in front of us. Lucia was now eighteen years old and pushing a sleeping Callum in a stroller that was perhaps too small for him. I threw the cigarette butt into the sea. I was annoyed by what was in front of me which made me remember where I was, in that simple world where you're born, you grow up, have kids, die, and everything is always the same. I told Enrico that I was cold and wanted to go back inside. I couldn't stand the strong smell coming from the piled-up fishing nets.

I got closer to walk by his side, the side without a crutch. I told him that he couldn't come to Giglio for a week and only see one corner of the port, so I proposed to show him another part.

"Are you interested in going on a trip tomorrow? I'll take you to read on other rocks, with another view. I'll show you the sunset from another side of the island—what do you think?"

"I think it's a great idea," he said to me, and without warning, I felt his hand touching my back and then going up towards the back of my neck, into my hair. "You're very beautiful."

In that wonderful moment, in which inebriation, fear, and waiting for pleasure all merged into a temporary but elusive happiness, I thought what a privilege it was to have a master key for every room.

I used it, without much delay, around three in the morning, when everything was silent, and I knew that there was someone waiting for me in Room 208. The stealth was a part of the game, the lights remained off, we kissed each other, we said things in a low voice that didn't need to be understood, he never took off his pajama pants, and he was very skillful in not making me feel the absence of his missing leg. You put a spell on me, he told me. I grabbed his warm hands and intertwined his fingers with mine. Time was suspended. I waited for him to sleep, watching his chest rise and fall in the penumbra of dawn, and I shivered at how unknown this man that I had just made love with was. I got dressed and, a bit before six, I was on the street, hiding myself under my ruffled hair from the looks of the fishermen and the baker, and, before arriving home where I would meet the most serious look of all from my mother, I cursed that shit hole, where secrets were within everyone's reach.

I didn't feel the need to justify my night out.

I showed up to the hotel in the afternoon. I found him at his usual spot reading and probably waiting for me. I sat close to him. He didn't touch me, just smiled.

I asked if he was still up for going on a trip to the light-house. He said, "Definitely."

I took Mom's Fiat Uno, and it made a loud screech as we pulled away, bringing to everyone's attention that I was leaving with a guest from the hotel. We began to laugh. I really liked this Enrico. There was something about him that fascinated me, beyond his intelligence, his accent, his beautiful eyes, and the fact that he was a man and not a boy. There was something else about him that moved me, and it had to do with a certain something in the wrinkles of certain expressions, like a restrained childish astonishment.

We arrived at Capel Rosso while the sun was setting. I parked on the dirt road in front of the entrance to the foot-path. I was nervous because I wanted at all costs for the moment to not be like when he had seen Ischia or Pantelleria, or when he rented a moped to see Santorini from the highest point. I wanted that open landscape, the vineyards by the sea and the old red and white lighthouse, to be, for him, as it was for me, a moment of pure marvel, the most beautiful place in the world. But he was not me and mine was a hopeless hope.

Waves of flowery and brackish air arrived so full that for long moments their smell dominated all other senses and it seemed that we couldn't see or hear each other very well. Enrico's prosthetic leg, which made us limp together, became more noticeable, the limping rhythm deafened, compelling us to stop and sit down on a block of granite to kiss, as if there were nothing else to do. I pushed his hair back so that he could feel the wind better. Everything around us was lit by the light of the sunset. I felt giddy with happiness, Enrico made me for-get about myself, my recent pain, everything about my life that I didn't like.

After the sun had completely set, I took him back to the port for his last dinner with his sister and brother-in-law, whom he felt he had neglected. I didn't join them: it didn't seem appropriate to dine out together. The following morning, I would have to check them out, and what would happen after I didn't have the strength to think about. I needed to return to Rome in two days. I wondered if I liked to put myself in ambiguous and heartbreaking situations, if I purposefully played games up until the last minute to leave open the possibilities for alibis and far-fetched hypotheses, easier than to face real life, which never spares you from the disappointment of how things really are, naked, in broad day, perhaps missing a leg and with a barren heart.

I got ready for bed, spinning the master key in my hand in anticipation of the moment.

Before Enrico returned to Milan, we exchanged emails and phone numbers. But everything that I'd imagined—messages of intense longing, recalling pleasures and wonder, packages of books, and train rides between Milan and Rome—died almost immediately. After his second laconic response to an excited message from me, I mitigated my expectations.

Before giving up, I tried to imagine stories about him, to fill the voids in which I could not find peace. Maybe he was married with kids and couldn't allow himself to be swept up by a new love. Maybe someone else read his emails and he didn't want to, or couldn't, risk it. Maybe he was scared of disappointment. I had his and his sister's personal information. I went to research his name on the Internet and news related to the university popped up. On websites for different scientific communities, through random combinations of search criteria, something popped up that I began to daydream about.

There had been a boy inside the Agricultural Bank, the day of the Piazza Fontana bombing, named Enrico, with an older sister named Patrizia. In that moment, when the information about their names and ages connected to that event, I felt my blood run cold. Their last name was different, but maybe, to maintain a certain discretion, they had changed it. From that moment on, my infatuation wasn't just with his charm, the deep seriousness of his intelligence, and his mysterious way of being. Suddenly, I had confirmation that he was the big event that I had never experienced in my life, that would give it the sort of tragic depth that it lacked, the pedestal of awful experiences that my mother and grandmother had lived through but that I had never been able to reach.

The secret that had to do with our lives, our childhood traumas, the things we didn't know how to say and which no one else had the courage to, a personal secret mixed with a series of horrendous State secrets, could be the thing that bonded us. I worked out a precise version of the facts. Enrico had lost his leg in the terrorist attack. I pretended to have been there too, to know that it happened that way.

Enrico has finished his homework on the still-set kitchen table, under the light of the decorated tree. He needs to go downtown with his sister before sunset, they need to run some errands at the bank, he doesn't know much, Patrizia is in charge. It is important that they do it quickly so Mom and Dad can join them to buy Enrico's Christmas present: soccer cleats. Enrico can't think about anything other than the moment when the sports store employee pushes down on the tip of his big toe and tells him that the size is perfect for him. Patrizia is ready: she puts on the brown coat that Mom wore the year before, and the hat and scarf her grandmother made for her. She has the body of a sudden puberty—she's the same as she was a few months ago, the girl with light eyes and long, dull hair, but some parts of her have grown more quickly than others: her neck, her nose, her breasts, which she hides by hunching over. She goes to the kitchen door and tells Enrico to hurry up. He puts on his jacket and pulls the zipper all the way up, puts on the wool cap that itches his forehead, and looks at his sister seriously with transparent eyes, as if to say: I can't go any faster. Enrico and Patrizia go out holding hands, but at the streetcar stop, they let go because they are now grown. They greet a client from their family's laundromat while looking at their feet. When the streetcar arrives, they sit in the back. Enrico puts his head between his knees so that he can see the road passing under them. On the fogged window he writes GO INTER, and the letters drip down in watery streams. When they get downtown it's after three. They are overwhelmed by the smell of chestnuts, by the flashing lights that shine in the fog. They take Corso Vittorio towards Il Barba. A crowd circulates slowly inside and out, the girl waits for her brother to detach from the candy shop's window, in which he sees his awkward, brown reflection. She tugs him; she doesn't want to be late. She needs to get to the bank as early as possible, because on Fridays it is always packed, and they need to be out of there by four-thirty. It begins to drizzle, and it seems to get darker with every step, a strange grey darkness that does not feel like night. The girl pushes the heavy door, and they enter the lobby of the bank that smells of smoke and heavy clothes, the kind under which people sweat. They find themselves in the circular hall overlooked by the teller counters and the glass partitions on the upper floor. In the middle of the rotunda is a large, octagonal, mahogany table covered by a plate of glass. On every side of the table is a chair, and on every chair sits at least one person surrounded by many others, standing. Patrizia makes her way through the crowd of people to reach a counter. They get in line. Enrico distracts himself. Two men next to him talk about a farm with fourteen cows. Enrico thinks about last summer in the mountains when a farmer made him attempt to milk a cow. He looks at the ground. He pictures the cleats on his feet and then sees them explode. A boom pierces his ears. He sees Patrizia's hat fly away, her hair dyed red, he feels the weight of her body fall on top of him and makes out the man with the cows whose face and jacket are now drenched by a stream of very dark blood. Now Enrico is on the floor. While lying down, he notices that where the table was, in the middle of the hall, there is now a smoking pile of wood, shards of glass, burnt flesh, and other things, that the stained-glass window overlooking Piazza Fontana is gone, and that everything outside is black, even though the lights are on. He sees something else dark, a coat maybe, burning and moving closer to him. Then the pain in his leg becomes stronger than anything else and all he sees is black.

When Silvana and Augusto get out of the car, which they parked on Via Larga to pick up Enrico and Patrizia, they realize something's not right. In the air, the overlapping sounds of sirens and a persistent burning smell. Silvana grabs her husband's jacket and starts walking faster. She doesn't say anything but begins to feel a discomfort building up inside her, something stronger than worry, that becomes more real with every step that takes her closer to the place where they were supposed to meet. Before turning the corner to see the exploded insides of the National Agricultural Bank, Silvana is certain that something terrible has happened to her children; the glare of the blue lights strobing on the wet sidewalk underlines her only words, a bradycardic whisper: no, no, no. When she gets to Piazza Fontana, Augusto sees her run towards a Carabiniere, throw herself at him, yell something about her children, look under every white sheet at the mutilated and charred dead bodies, stick her nails into her hands, and say, "Maybe they're at the Fatebenefratelli Hospital," then fall silent, her face white with terror. Two Carabinieri take them in their car. Along the way, no one says a thing. The noise of the siren overlays Silvana's nos while Augusto, with his glasses fogged up and his hands crossed, continues to say the beginning of Lord's Prayer *to himself, without getting past "thy will be done." The Carabinieri drive up to the emergency room and escort them to the head nurse on duty, who takes too long to understand that these two don't need to be treated but are the parents of the two children that arrived by ambulance. One second too long of that misunderstanding and Silvana has already grabbed the nurse by the collar of her gown. "I WANT TO KNOW WHERE MY CHILDREN ARE." "Please calm down, ma'am. They are in surgery. The girl is in women's surgery and the boy in orthopedic. Let me take you to the doctors, they will be able to tell you more." They talk about wounds and burns for Patrizia, the removal of a foreign body from her arm, a problem with Enrico's right leg, but Silvana only hears the most beautiful words ever said to her: non-life-threatening injuries. She looks in her wallet for some change to call her mother, with the haste one has when there is bad news.*

When Enrico opens his eyes, the first thing he focuses on is the photo of the Pope on the back wall, with an olive branch tucked behind the frame, and then the IV. He's been trying to fully wake up for more than six hours. He has a terrible taste in his mouth, his throat burns. His grandmother is nearby. "Enrico," she says, stroking his hand resting on the bedspread. He's unable to focus on his thoughts; he begins to repeat, "I'm thirsty." His grandmother is forbidden to let him drink because of the anesthesia. He falls back asleep, complaining. His grandmother wipes his dry lips with the edge of a handkerchief soaked in water. The second time he wakes up he hears his grandmother calling his name again. He focuses on the doorway: there are two men dressed in black, one tall, the other with a mustache. "Come on in," his grandmother says, "he's awake now." The taller one asks, "Are you sure we're not a bother?" Without understanding what could've brought them to the foot of his bed, Enrico says their names: "Mazzola . . . Facchetti . . ." The two get closer to him. The boy tries to sit up without success, the grandmother and the one with the mustache help him up. "How are you?" the tall one asks. Without giving time for a response, he places a package in Enrico's hands. "This is for you, from everybody on the team." Enrico doesn't have the strength to open it, his grandmother does it for him. It's a black and blue striped Inter Milan jersey, with the number 10 on the back. He doesn't believe that he's actually awake. His idols came to visit him, and they brought him a signed jersey. He's able to say, "Thank you," with a faint voice. Facchetti tells him that they came behind their coach's back, and they need to go because the team has an away match. While forcing himself to listen, Enrico looks down at the bed and notices the strange shape of his body under the covers. He tries to move his feet. Something moves, but only on his left side. He looks at Mazzola and Facchetti. He's no longer listening to them. He stares at the flat side of the bed. The two soccer players didn't even take off their coats. Facchetti ruffles Enrico's hair before leaving. "We'll let you rest now, it's best." Enrico closes his eyes and raises his hand to say goodbye only after it's too late. He says, "Nonna," and after a long pause, "let me look under the covers." His grandmother doesn't want to. She tries to change the subject, "Enrico you have a fever, try to sleep a little." "I said let me look under the covers." His grandmother lowers her head and raises the bed-sheet and cover on top, with a firm gesture. Enrico only has on a hospital gown and underwear. His eyes remain closed. He tries to rotate his feet inwards, he clearly feels the movement, his toes touch each other. Now he opens his eyes. And he sees. His right leg ends in a white knot of gauze, held together by an elastic net, at his knee.

Between the grandmother's eyes and the grandson's face, space and time no longer exists. They both feel the same pain. For a moment, the silence becomes a dense liquid that inhibits their breathing, that prevents any movement. Enrico throws his head back and does the strangest thing: he smiles. Then he whispers to his grandmother: "Tell me who did it." There isn't any air in her throat, in a lump are tied up the words that she wanted to say to him, "I don't know who did it, Enrico, but if I find out, I'll kill them with my own two hands." But all she did with those same hands was pull the covers back over him and caress his burning forehead.

I had created the whole story and convinced myself of it. I gave it one last try. I hoped that by sharing a secret with me, he would finally open the door to his heart.

I wrote him a long message, in which I talked about what I'd been doing since I returned to Rome, ending with the fact that I had attended an anniversary dinner with some people who were a part of the Giglio uprisings of '76, when the islanders tried to drive Freda and Ventura out from their confinement on the island. I told him about how the Piazza Fontana bombing was, along with Nonna's stories of the Resistance, the historical event that scared me the most when I was little. I asked him if he remembered anything about it, since he would have been a preteen.

He responded with this: "Teresa, you have a very vivid imagination. I know why you asked me those questions at the end of your email. Once and for all: Patrizia and I are not Patrizia and Enrico Pizzamiglio from the Agricultural Bank. We have the same names and we're about the same age, and it's true, I have lost a leg like Enrico Pizzamiglio. It's a strange coincidence that has led to more than one misunderstanding about my life and my sister's, but it's still just a coincidence. At the time of Piazza Fontana, we weren't even in Milan, because we lived in Vimercate, in Brianza. My leg had to be amputated when I was seventeen because of a tumor. I know that it would've been more heroic and symbolic to lose it in the attack. You're curious about me, Teresa, I understand, but there's no reason to be, there's nothing special about me. I'm just a disabled, lonely professor, with thick glasses, always hunched over numbers and books, older than you by ten years.

You have the sun in you, and you deserve someone as bright as you are by your side. Not a distant black hole. The time we spent together in Giglio was unforgettable, but I'm sure that there are many men more worthy than me to whom you can direct your light and wonderful attention. Be well and say hello to the island for me."

I didn't respond to him. I shut down the computer and before even thinking about it, I had a good cry. I processed his humiliating response, I convinced myself he was right, that it wasn't worth it, and I began to build a nice castle of cauterizing distractions over this new wound. Friends, eating out, and a weekend in Paris with Caterina, who called me a mythomaniac when I told her the story of the Piazza Fontana coincidence. Work, work, work, tight deadlines, focus groups, and stomachaches all over again.

Three weeks of intensive shock therapy and I was over it. My life and Enrico's had quickly crossed paths and just as quickly they resumed their course, two parallel lines like those that appeared, purple, on my pregnancy test, after being ten days late.

22.

It was the life inside me that made me understand the value of my own. That test, which I took after a night of drinking, was the most enlightening epiphany of my almost thirty-year existence. Astonishment, as if it could never happen to me, soon gave way to certainty: my life was necessary not only for me but also to fulfill another. Only I carried that life within me, and it made me unique and absolute.

I had been so busy for so long internalizing the fact of my inferiority, making myself invisible, making myself forgettable, surrendering myself to the fact that others did not recognize my autonomy or that they did well to decide for me. What use had I made of my own freedom up until that moment? I had used it to make everyone else happy. Now it was time to make myself happy. Now I would come first.

I wasn't going to let anyone tell me to have an abortion. I wasn't going to tell Enrico, who at most would have accompanied me to a clinic and then sent me home with sincere greetings to the island. I wasn't going to tell my mom, who would have surely disapproved. I wasn't going to tell Caterina, who would have subtly manipulated me, convincing me to do what she would have done in my situation in order not to ruin her life. I was going to be the one to choose, for myself and for my child. I felt powerful. I hid my pregnancy for the first three months so I could share the news once it would be too late to listen to the many voices that would advise me to not keep the baby.

I decided to break my silence towards the end of November, when I was already thirteen weeks along. The nausea had completely passed, and I felt better than ever. I had a great book on the phases of pregnancy: now the little one already had all of their organs formed: skin, nails, microscopic baby teeth inside their gums. With my secret hidden in my womb, I took a train to see Mom and Nonna, who were in Orbetello for the winter.

But before that I had called Caterina. I wanted her to be the first to know. I had anticipated her response: "What the fuck did you just say?" The insults that were mixed with sincere emotion, the lecture about how I was medieval, that there was birth control, the reproach for not telling her earlier, almost as if she had been usurped of her primacy over my life, her way of putting herself first before everything.

"The baby is that cripple's from Piazza Fontana, right?"

"Yes, but it's not his. It's mine."

"Are you thinking of not telling him anything?"

"You should forget about his existence too. He doesn't

want anything to do with me; imagine how he would feel about a child."

"He could help you financially."

"No. I'm not interested in my child having an ATM for a father or in forcing someone who doesn't want a child to have one. Let's act as if I'm the Madonna, that this child is a gift from God and it's a gift for me."

"Saint Teresa of Avila! You've suddenly become a believer? These hormones are making you crazy. Maybe you should tell the father anyway. You can't be sure how he's going to react. You can't decide for him. And the child will probably want a father. Maybe a long-distance father is better than no father."

"I've thought about it a lot, Cate, really. Maybe it's a selfish choice, and maybe I'm shooting myself in the foot. But I don't want to share the responsibility with anyone, especially with someone who certainly doesn't have the slightest intention of becoming a father or starting a family with me and who might blame me for my whole life because they think it was a mistake. This new life for me is a precious gift after Dad's death. I can't stand someone reducing it all to a stupid mistake. I'm twenty-nine, I have a job, and many people to help me. What's to stop me from having this baby now? I already love it."

My sister honored me with her truth: "Teresa, you are truly one of a kind. You're the only person I know who can find beauty even in the bad. You're like someone who's been given a treasure map, but loses their way because they got distracted, digs in a random spot, finds a piece of quartz and thinks it's the treasure. Your child will be a lucky baby: they'll have a mother with the talent of finding happiness. And a smart aunt and grandmother for everything else."

There it was, they were there for everything else. Mine was only an abstract talent. She was already letting me know that I wouldn't be able to do it alone.

To my amazement, Nonnalina was the only one who reacted

unexpectedly. I had predicted almost verbatim what the other women in the family would say. I expected from my mom: "You are irresponsible. You absolutely must inform the baby's father. How do you think you can do it alone? I won't be able to help you between the hotel and Nonna. Forget it, I'm coming to Rome." She said it all except the last sentence, and only after giving me a hug and crying with emotion. It was her personal form of joy, always wrapped up in a shroud of worry and pessimism. Nonnalina nodded in silence. She didn't seem happy at all. She looked like someone who wanted to say, "Oh God, another problem. Nothing ever goes right in this family." But before I left for Rome, she took me aside. "Teresa, I'm very happy to become a great-grandmother. It is a beautiful thing. You know, I had to raise your mother by myself: I was younger than you and I had lost everything, my husband, parents, brothers, in-laws. I didn't have a house, I didn't have a job, I didn't have an education. But I did it. In fact, having the baby was my salvation, it pushed me to try my best, to do everything I could to provide for her. And despite the sacrifices and the exhaustion, raising Elena, making her study, was the thing that made me most happy, that saved me. Go your own way, Teresa, and don't be afraid. You're good, you're intelligent, you have an education, you have a job although I don't understand what it is yet. You don't necessarily need a man close by to raise a child. We are not the kind of women who need men around. We manage ourselves. It's our destiny. She will be beautiful, you'll see. She'll be a girl too. I'm only sorry that I'm too old to help you, but I'll visit sometimes and take care of the baby while you go to the office. And in Giglio, you know, don't you? They'll gossip, they'll say mean things because you don't have a husband. Don't listen to anyone, they're just townies with nothing to do. Say that the child's father is a sailor, then they'll all be scared. I'm joking, dear, after they gossip for a little, they'll find something else to talk about. And whoever loves you will always love you. Look how beautiful you are—you have never looked this beautiful, even your hair is more voluminous."

I hugged her without trying to hold back my tears. I was wrong that there was only one person who believed in me and I had lost him. There was still Nonnalina.

I was more and more sure of what I was doing. And that year needed a bright spot. I was taken by the idea that for a lost father, I deserved a child, someone to love, as a reward, as if life and death were a zero-sum game.

PART IV
(2011 – 2012)

23.

In the end, I named the baby Lorenzo. I learned at the second ultrasound that it was a boy and I was blown away, because I always thought of another little girl in our family of women. I had to get used to the idea, project myself into a future of toy cars and balls for which I was not ready.

For the rest of the pregnancy I had insisted on "Vittorio," even if the name was becoming less common and sounded vaguely fascist, which no one liked. A few minutes after the birth, full of hormonal turmoil, I began to feel afraid that giving my son my father's name would awaken nostalgia for him every time I spoke to the child. Lorenzo was a beautiful name, and the patron saint of Porto.

I knew immediately, I understood it the moment I held him to my chest while he was still attached to the cord, amazed that he'd been born healthy and with two legs (I never confessed to anyone that while I was pregnant I was convinced that a Lamarckian phenomenon was taking place and the child would inherit his father's disability): this child cries with desperation, his crying isn't like the others'. He is different from me. He grieves, he screams things with extra anger. He will push my willpower.

The months of my pregnancy in Rome had been beautiful. My belly was like an airbag between me and the problems of the world: the more it grew, the more it distanced us and protected me. Trouble at work, the hysteria of the clients and of my boss, my colleagues' whining, the political issues of this corrupt country in the hands of incompetent fools—all bounced off my protruding belly and didn't scratch me in any way. Classical music, organic food, cinema. I had forbidden my mother to talk to me about Berlusconi. That sense of tranquility never returned. A magical period that ended with preeclampsia and an emergency C-section for which no one was prepared. Anna, the friend who lived closest to me, came with me. There he was, the baby that would absorb my every thought and all the time I had. I remember the nights I stayed awake to watch his breathing, the bonding moments of breastfeeding every two or three hours. The obsession over whether he ate enough, hoping that he would grow up to meet the expectations that he had been born with. The tiny closed nose that kept him from sucking well, the stump of the umbilical cord that didn't heal when it was supposed to. So many worries. And then the rest of the world disappeared suddenly, even from sight: while I was breastfeeding my myopia increased, I saw nothing beyond what I held in my arms and I didn't care. I finally felt important, truly indispensable. I was the food that ensured life. By fulfilling my biological duty, both of us were born: the little Lorenzo and the adult Teresa. I was exhausted, experienced back pain, I was always tired, but I felt strong, satisfied. And obviously, for that form of happiness, there would be a price to pay.

My grandmother had a terrible life, my mother a little less so, but to improve things even that little bit was hard, and she had to work like crazy. I don't know much about the ancestors who preceded them, but I imagine that they didn't do well at all. Looking back at my family's past through the matrilineal branch, I always had the impression that, as in Greek tragedies, someone had committed a mortal sin of *hubris* that had to be repented for seven generations, after which, with decades of wars and misfortunes having passed, we could begin to live again. When I was in high school and studying Euripides, I was sure that I'd been born in the eighth generation that had the task of restoring happiness, according to the hierarchy of inheritance that *hubris* prescribed. But it was a difficult task that would require tremendous effort.

Perhaps it's not the pain itself but the memory of the pain that is inherited. And it is the furrow in which we take our first steps, sometimes without realizing that the furrow becomes a well-worn road. And the feelings of guilt on this road are holes, deeper than those dug from pain. I too have always felt I had to pay in some way, and maybe I had gladly accepted the fact that raising a child alone might be enough recompense.

And I was alone, even though my mom always supported me, especially during Lorenzo's first year, and whenever she could, in the winter, she came to my house, a small house, in Monteverde, where I had only one bedroom and there was always too little space to contain Lorenzo's whims, my feelings of guilt, and Red's complaints, who would do anything for her grandchild but never actually enjoyed him. She was so busy feeding him, putting him to sleep, washing him, and taking care of him that in the end she was too tired to play with him, laugh with him, observe him while he tried everything for the first time. And even if she had stopped saying so, the undertones were clear: once again she had to bear the worst consequences of a family member's irresponsible choice.

And then during the summers in Giglio, Lorenzo spent half his time wearing floaties at the beach with his great-grandmother under the palm trees of San Lorenzo, while I worked in the hotel that bore his name. Lorenzo grew up like this, surrounded by the love of women and excessive attention. Few diversions, two places, two macro-seasons, two horizons that I hadn't been able to stand for a long time and, which in the end, became one.

We had overcome many things, the boy born in the new millennium and I. Countless disapproving looks (for having a pacifier for too long, for our shared surname that betrayed the absence of a father, for too many gifts at Christmas, and too few male role models), about twenty epic lectures from Red, (loving but never missing the opportunity to make me feel like I was living out my destiny of pre-ordained disappointment), men attempting to hit on me a dozen times at school (because if a woman does not have a partner, she is definitely "easy"), ten alternatives for arts and craft projects for Father's Day.

By sixth grade he swam like a dolphin and had a ton of friends who came round in the evening. He was good at math and had blue eyes, an above average intelligence—beautiful things not from my DNA. I always told him many stories, as Caterina had with me, and when he asked about his father I told him that he was in heaven, that there had been an accident. And when, a little older, he asked me if I had a picture of him, I told him no, in the previous century there were still no digital cameras or cellphones and we hadn't taken a photo in time, but I described him to Lorenzo and told him that if he wanted to get an idea of what he looked like he could watch a famous talk show with me where one of the hosts vaguely resembled him.

"Okay," he said to me watching it, "so he looks like anyone with a beard and nerdy glasses."

"Your father had a limp too."

"What strange taste you have, Mom."

24.

One evening I drove to pick him up from his friend Giulio's. His mom had invited me to stay for dinner, but I didn't feel like doing so; my hands began to tremble on the wheel. I pulled over, called them, and asked if they could keep Lorenzo for dinner. I would have to pick him up afterwards because something had come up last minute at work.

What had come up was that I no longer had a job. That afternoon I had been called into Marinella's office. She was the owner of Marketest, where I'd worked for almost fifteen years. I seemed to be unable to recognize her voice as she told me that the company was doing poorly, that we had been operating at a loss for two years, no one had any money for market research, that we were no longer competitive, that we had not been for a long time, could I perhaps imagine how long?

And here, even though I had remained silent, she had raised her voice, as if she wanted to reproach me for not knowing such a simple answer. "For ten years! And do you know what these ten years overlap with? With Lorenzo's age, since you haven't been able to give all of yourself to the research, in fact not even half of yourself, since you started to pull away, unable to work overtime, staying home when the child was sick." After that she went on about the optional maternity leave, such a good initiative for women, but what about the entrepreneurs who were left without staff? Plus the four weeks in August when I went to Giglio and she had to hire another person because my limited time was not enough. I sat more and more silent and motionless in the chair. "I didn't fire you earlier out of compassion, so as to not leave you on the street with your son, out of a sense of responsibility I have for you and that you never had for me, seeing that you never put your heart into your work, you never truly cared about the research outcomes or finding new clients or doing anything that wasn't the bare minimum to earn your paycheck at the end of the month. But now I'm the one who can't sleep at night! I can't do it anymore. I can't allow it. We can't allow it." Gradually, her outburst faded; we had reached the climax with "you never put your heart into your work," Marinella's voice had lowered, my faults had become those of the market. I must have looked miserable.

"Now things are going badly and the government certainly doesn't help us. I just can't do half your job anymore, which is a huge burden, and costs twice as much as two full-time employees. I have to make cuts, do you understand? There's no other option. I have to bet everything on my work and on Sabrina, who is younger and childless and has time to do the things you can't anymore. I gritted my teeth and tightened my belt for as long as I could and it hurts my heart, because I love you, I love you and Lorenzo, but if I keep on like this, I'll have to fold, and I have to think about my children, too . . ."

Three seconds of silence.

Then she started up again. "You still have three months, you can stay until summer. I'll write you an excellent reference letter; you'll have time to find a new job without stress. I'm sure that, as bright as you are, it won't take long for you to be hired by a larger company. Maybe you'll find a well paid part-time job. That would be ideal for you and Lorenzo."

I couldn't manage to say anything. So I did something my father would have done. I got up and I took from the wall the Pink Enterprise Prize from the Province of Rome awarded to

Marketest
Marinella Giunti
Model of Female Entrepreneurship

and, smashing it repeatedly with three, four sharp blows, I broke it on the desk, even cutting my finger. I saw Marinella's horrified face, horrified and satisfied for having done the right thing and receiving confirmation that firing me was truly a necessity given my psychological state. I left pleased with my dramatic and liberating gesture, satisfied by the fact that in that moment, I had fulfilled the most powerful symbolic event of my life, since Marketest's Pink Enterprise Prize was now stained with the red of my blood.

I left Marinella's office and left the door open behind me. I turned off my computer, took my bag, and left. I drove aimlessly for two hours in the car. The traffic in Rome was the ideal place to experience a moment like this: Rome's traffic is already a simmering broth of rage and I was only one of the ingredients that was boiling in it, just like the others. In my head, I repeated everything that I had wanted to say to Marinella, a string of obscenities in which fuck-yous and the local Tuscan curses alternated with accusations of the horrendous hypocrisy of your fucking female-led business, which was only successful because women always let themselves be exploited more easily, and a rundown of all the lunches I'd eaten in front of the computer in order to be able to leave earlier, at least for a good reason, to pick up my child from school, and not to go get a French manicure like you, bitch. And you know, I'll tell you that you're absolutely right when you say that I never put my heart into this job because, unlike you, I use my heart for important things, not for shitty market research. You know what, Marinella, I'm genuinely happy, happy to be rid of you and this job that I always hated, along with the focus groups that only served to make you money. Marinella, Marinella, what a great favor you did me. I would have never had the courage, but you lifted a huge weight off my chest. I can tell you in complete honesty that I hated that job, that office, and you, Marinella. I hope, like the song by Fabrizio de André says, you fall into the river, now that it's spring.

25.

I confess that that evening, overwhelmed by despair, by the terror of not being able to give my son a decent future, I searched on the Internet to find his father. I had only done it once before, in May 2005, during the final sentencing for the Piazza Fontana massacre, after thirty-seven years and dozens of trials and thousands and thousands of pages of investigations, which confirmed the definitive acquittal of the defendants and the obligation of the victims' families to pay for the legal costs. It was a day I will never forget. I was so indignant, I wanted to call him to hear what he thought and offer condolences. Because he *was* the little boy from the Agricultural Bank, I was sure of it. I had never believed the story about the tumor. My son is the son of a victim and will never know his father. He grew up with extraordinary strength, like my mother, the daughter of a martyr to the Resistance, and has extra courage transmuted by others' pain.

It was easy to find Enrico's new contact information. He hadn't lost his job: he always ended up teaching somewhere. The most recent trace of him was among the teachers of the mathematics department at Stanford University in California. I wrote down the number and email on a little piece of paper that I put in the change pocket of my wallet. Then I called my sister. I told her everything through tears.

"Caterina, I can no longer live here in Rome with Lorenzo without a salary, do you understand?"

"Teresa, for the twentieth consecutive year I repeat: COME-TO-PA-RIS. You'll learn French right away, you can find a job, schools, subsidies for single parents, everything, everything's here, I'm here to help you out, I really don't understand what's holding you back, you know Paris well by now, I'm sure Lorenzo would be excited. So would I, to have my little nephew here. You'd be giving him a great gift. It takes much more courage to stay in Italy these days than to pick up and leave."

"Caterina, I swear that this time I'll think about it seriously. But it's not that easy. Learning enough French to be able to work there someplace that isn't a McDonald's, it's not that easy for me these days and . . . Lorenzo isn't that young anymore. He's happy here, he has his friends, his school, his language. And then there's Mom and Nonna . . ."

"These are all minor problems compared to the fact that you can't stay in Rome without work, so you have to make a decision. Either find work quickly or do something else. And the time has arrived for you to do something else, make a better choice, do the thing you've been putting off for years with rather cowardly excuses."

"It's not the excuses that are cowardly, it's me."

"I'll tell you just one last thing, with all the sisterly love that I have: the biggest mistake you could make would be to return to Giglio."

The next morning, Lorenzo focused those blue eyes on me while he dipped his cookies in milk.

"Mom, why are your eyes so swollen? Were you crying?"

"Yes."

"Is it because you lost your job?"

"Yes."

"Is it true that it's my fault that you lost it?"

"What are you saying, Lori, no! I lost it because there is a crisis, because there are no clients, businesses don't have any more money for research and there's a lot of competition."

"But Marinella told you that ever since I was born, you haven't worked anymore. She fired you because you came to my swim race. I told you that it didn't matter, that Giulio's mother could take me."

"How do you know that? Who told you these things?"

"I heard you saying them on the phone last night."

"What, you spied on me?"

"No, you were shouting. It was impossible not to hear you."

"Lorenzo, there are complicated things in adulthood and

one of them is being a parent and working. But the last thing I want you to do, the absolute last, is to think that it's your fault. You don't have to worry about anything. I lost a job that I didn't like and in the end I'm happy about it. I'm only angry about how I was fired. But I'll find a nicer one and maybe we will go and live in Paris."

"I don't want to go to Paris."

"Why? It's so beautiful! And your aunt is there."

"It is beautiful, but there are too many French people. And their food is bad. It rains and the sea is far away. It's not my home. Here we have everything, Mom, we are so well, you, me, and our friends."

I didn't care that he was grown up now and didn't want to be touched. I hugged him and kissed his hair. He stood still and was aware of his power. I dropped him off at school and then came back home to sleep. I kept my phone off for the whole day. In the afternoon, I took Lorenzo to Villa Pamphili for him to play soccer with his classmates while I stood reading under a pine tree in the sun until they had finished. It would be nice if I never had to work again.

26.

But work was necessary. We waited for the end of school and moved to Giglio for the summer, renting out the house in Rome, to help my mom who couldn't handle it alone anymore, with Nonnalina always on her heels; Nonnalina had started to live in the clouds and her only point of reference was her daughter's red hair. At that point Red's hair was dyed, and from Occhetto onwards she had also ceased to be a communist (because it was no longer worth it, she said, watered down ideologies in service of whomever wanted to keep their seats), metamorphosing instead into a fervent anti-Berlusconist.

Another season began in the worst way. I was not in the right mood to deal with clients. I was not in the right mood for anything. I went to Caterina's in Paris for a week at the end of June. She was a professor at the École des Beaux-arts and she continued to write for various publications, but her job was constantly under threat from the enormous load of new, competitive recruits who were elbowing their way into the spotlight. She wasn't old enough to be considered a professor, but she wasn't young enough to shine with the light of promising genius she had enjoyed when she first arrived in the city. To maintain her position she was constrained to a life of presenteeism. Hervé was merciless about it. By then he was very well-known and his partner had to be at his level. He was counting on the fact that Caterina would sooner or later become the *eminence grise* of contemporary art, but he was annoyed that she was struggling more than expected. Hervé was building his life like a ladder-shaped sculpture whose rungs were the people that mattered—other artists, journalists, poets, architects, writers—and gradually he climbed. And the more he climbed, the more he realized that he was still too low, because sometimes he was able to see normal people close to him, people who really ruined the composition of the piece, people like his sister-in-law who disturbed the ambiance of his living room with clothes that were too colorful, and disrupted *Lucia di Lammermoor* with a loud voice that was wasted on phrases that were never quotable, in a language that he knew very poorly and was only good for singing.

Hervé therefore tried not to see me. He avoided me and didn't say hello while I was in Paris. He disappeared into his atelier.

Caterina tried to protect me; she told me that she had kicked Hervé out during the day so the two of us could have some peace and quiet. We had breakfast together, then I joined her during her lunch break and we walked to the Jardin des

Plantes, where she lectured me about being too easily satisfied. The evenings, however, belonged to Hervé.

"I have to be with him, otherwise he gets anxiety attacks; it's how he is, like a kid." She smiled while she said it and I wondered why she had taken on the mission of having to bear him, and why she didn't protect herself from his lack of love and how she could be happy living a life made of all that scaffolding, in service to a megalomaniac who was a slave to his reputation, who looked at her sideways, who questioned everything.

I felt pity for her loneliness and rage over the way she endured Hervé by pretending to herself that she was actually a sort of factotum mother and that she had everything under control. I was thankful for the willpower that had prevented me from calling Enrico. I was thankful that I didn't have a penny and no one to tell me what to do or what not to do, whom I should hang out with and which jacket to wear. I was thankful to have Lorenzo. I was thankful for the ridiculous and touching gifts that he brought home from school trips. Caterina was right, I was too easily satisfied. Of the two of us, I remained the second, the youngest in every way, the one who had lost the battle to establish herself, to escape provincialism, to emancipate herself, trapped as I was by needs, but I was still happy, for the umpteenth time in my life, that I wasn't her.

I went back to Giglio without a shred of a plan for the future. My sister was right. It was easy to choose the less risky solution. I was going to stay there: at least I had a job and a house and I would be able to decide what to do next by taking some time for myself. The frustration I felt was bad for my state of mind.

In recent years, to return to Giglio in August was akin to discovering a betrayal. And no matter how hard I tried to forgive this, nothing was ever the same. It had become difficult for me to stand the lack of gratitude of the islanders for the long Campese sunsets or for the tourists who had spared them from pulling trammel nets up at sunrise, from the thirst of vegetable gardens barely surviving among the granite. The summer island became the kingdom of no love. For the people of Giglio, the rush to make a few months' pay that would last them all year became the only reason to live. In their eyes downcast on the cash registers, in their missed smiles, one could read all their annoyance over having those strangers around.

In this way, I really felt like them: I had a bad temper and I didn't do anything to force the kindness that didn't come spontaneously.

One evening a group from Verona asked me to organize a tour around the island for the next day. In cases like this I would call Pietro, who had a big boat on which he also offered lunch, and who was always short on money. Deirdre had left a couple of years earlier to take Callum with her to Ireland. She had no intention of returning to Giglio and Pietro began the life of a separated father with a distant son: he spent everything he had on travel and child support. In the winter he had to set off on his boat again. When he could, he worked as a skipper on charter boats that left for cruises in the Mediterranean, sometimes to the Caribbean.

The group of Veronese returned in the evening with a series of complaints. The boat was uncomfortable, the sea was too rough, lunch on board was scant, the cutlery was dirty, they didn't understand why they couldn't get off on Campese beach, one of them had thrown up and Pietro didn't take her ashore. I said I was sorry, the weather hadn't helped because the seas were a bit rough, and I added that life on a boat doesn't have the comforts of a hotel. The one with the bald, sunburned head said to me: "With what we spent, we could have gone on a cruise." I threw a hundred-euro bill at him. "Go on a cruise next year. Giglio is too extreme a vacation for people like you." He called me rude, but pocketed the hundred euros quickly.

Then I called Pietro. I told him that if he treated people badly, I wouldn't send them to him anymore. He asked me what happened. I told him. He began to laugh. "It's not my fault they got seasick and expected a yacht with waiters. When they wanted me to bring the one who felt sick to shore, I explained that I wasn't allowed to get closer than the buoys, that it wasn't a life or death situation, and that if they really wanted, I could have called the lifeguard to pick them up on a pedal boat, but they didn't want to. What the fuck was I supposed to do?"

"Yes, but what about lunch and the dirty cutlery?"

"I made them pasta with clams. Bread, butter, and anchovies. Peaches and *panficato*. It was all good. No one has ever complained. Were they expecting silver cutlery? These people are badly behaved."

"No Pietro, we can't think we're always right. We should be more kind and guarantee impeccable service, understood? If you get paid like you do, I should never receive complaints. I had to give him a hundred euros back because of this."

"You're an idiot."

"Ah thank you, you can be sure that I'll send you more tourists."

"I'll see if I can manage . . . don't think my work depends on who you send me."

I hung up, determined not to let my blood boil. At night I went out to watch Lorenzo play a soccer match on the little beach on the harbor. I smoked a cigarette as I watched him run and throw himself in the sand all sweaty, ready to lecture him to take a shower before going to bed. While I crushed the butt on the fence wall, I felt something around my waist. It was Pietro.

"Come on, Teresa, don't be mad. I'm sorry about the group today. But they were really terrible, you know, people who complain about everything . . ."

"I know, they are unbearable shitheads, but . . ." And there, my anger dissolved. I felt like laughing. "The bald one who was all red is the worst . . . he changed rooms twice, first because of noise, and then because the window didn't close all the way . . ."

"These people never fuck, in my opinion."

"I almost want to prank them . . . you saw how ugly his daughter is, poor thing, she's probably ten years old and always cranky—nothing ever suits her, like her father," I continued.

"And why do you think I chose the route heading into the wind? . . . I rode straight into the waves so they'd hit them in their faces!"

And we laughed, like when we were young, not because these things were so funny, but because each other's laughter made us have fun regardless. There was something broken between us that could only be healed through that—a fleeting complicity that united us against someone else.

"Listen Tere, I'll give you back the hundred euros."

"No, come on, don't worry about it."

"Yes, it's my fault. I'll at least give you fifty."

"I don't want it."

"Okay, then let's go and get a drink. Are you up for it?"

"Just a gin and tonic because I have to wake up early tomorrow. If we find the Veronese, we can offer them drinks too."

"Of course. Grappa in dirty glasses. The house speciality."

I shouted at Lorenzo to be home by eleven and take a shower. He made a gesture with his arm that was more "go away" than "goodbye."

We sat at the lighthouse bar. Pietro went inside to get a drink without waiting for them to serve us. When he returned, Beatrice, the pharmacist's daughter, had already joined our table with two other girls in their thirties, one of whom was very tanned and well-groomed, who only spoke of pleasant things, as if her life was made out of a material that was impermeable to problems or sadness, and any subject that could not be talked about with joy was categorized as "heavyyyy." She drank until her extroversion turned into harassment. Since her target was Pietro, I left early. I had to go see if Lorenzo was home. Plus, my Birkenstocks, linen pants from the market, and the suffering and intolerance in my eyes excluded me from any competition. I was out. I was old.

Lorenzo was happy in Giglio over the summer, like all children given the opportunity to run around freely, come home whenever they want, spend the whole day with each other playing at the beach, forgetting about their parents but always finding a meal ready when hungry. He was happy in Giglio until I told him that we would not return to Rome in September and that he had to start seventh grade there, in Porto.

He looked at me as if I had punched him in the stomach. As if behind his back I'd planned a wickedness not worthy of a mother.

"You can't do this to me."

"Lorenzo, I understand that it's difficult, but it's only for a year: then we'll find a way to return to Rome. Or we'll go to Paris, but we won't stay here. I promise you that."

"I don't understand what's nice about being stuck here in the winter. Do you understand that there's nothing to do here? Can't you find another job in Rome?"

"It's increasingly difficult in Rome, and also I rented out the house."

"You rented out the house? So we can't even go back there? What about my stuff?"

"I put everything in storage, and we'll have it sent here."

"But why didn't you tell me any of this? You should have told me! Do I not matter?"

"You matter so much, Lorenzo, you matter more than anything else. I want to give you a beautiful life and in Rome, at the moment, it wouldn't have been . . . you'll see. When you grow up and you think of this year you'll thank me."

He began to cry. I hugged him and he broke free. He ran away and I saw that he went to the high rock. The place where we've tried to solve our problems for three generations, as if the answers came from the horizon.

Giglio had been something else when Vittorio was there. How could I explain it to my son so he could somehow find all that beauty? For me it was impossible. It was as if when he left, Vittorio had taken everything and turned off the lights before closing the door. I didn't know anyone anymore. My friends had left and the colors had also gone out. How could I expect my son to be happy?

He had to adapt. When he started school, he quickly realized that it was a way to pass time that he couldn't take seriously. There were twelve students in the entire middle school. Lorenzo did the eighth-grade curriculum: he could skip his homework and still be the best out of everyone. He had had it with me. He spent the whole day on the computer, chatting with his friends in Rome, always answering me rudely, and when I tried to involve him in my online French class, he told me to go to hell. I slapped him and confiscated anything with a screen. We didn't speak to each other for two days. Two days in which I lost sight of him. Not that I was worried. At least he left the house and detached himself from those infernal chats. The second evening he came home around seven with a sea bream that weighed more than a kilo.

"Who gave you this?"

"I caught it with Pietro! We went on his boat, yesterday and today. He taught me a lot of tricks, and look at this! So cool! Will you cook it for me tonight?"

I nodded happily and went out to buy potatoes. Upon

returning, I heard Lorenzo's cellphone chirping furiously. He had found it. I didn't say anything because he was sending photos of the fish to his friends and he was right to do so, because with a catch like this it was permissible to brag.

The next day I decided to go to the cafe for breakfast. I wanted to find out if they knew of a puppy to adopt. It would have made Lorenzo happy. He always asked me if he could have a dog, and since we couldn't have one in Rome, here in Giglio it would be the perfect new member of our small family. I knew I was breaking a promise I had made after Irma's death, but that was a different life.

I met with Pietro. I thanked him for the bream and he smiled sideways, telling me that Lorenzo had done everything. We sat down for coffee at the small table outside, next to the card players who had already started their day.

I was in a good mood. But Pietro and I had an argumentative exchange that spoiled it.

"Teresa, I'm sorry to ask you this, but does your son know who his father is? Has he ever met him?"

"No, but that's none of your damn business. I don't understand why you feel so entitled to ask me about something so personal. Did I ever ask you why Deirdre left you?"

"You could have. Aren't we still friends? I only ask because Lorenzo came looking for me. It seems that he really wants to be with an older male. That he's looking for a father figure. He told me you wanted him to take an online French course. You'll turn him into a fag!"

"What are you saying, Pietro! Who do you think you are? Do you mean to tell me that I'm not a good mother? And that you think you're a good father from thousands of miles away?"

"Calm down, I wasn't talking about you. I just wanted to say that Lorenzo, like all boys his age, needs to be with other men older than him, to learn things that you can't teach him."

"Okay, Freud of the beach! Maybe you're the one who misses your child and you're looking for a surrogate in mine? Either way, I don't want YOU to be his male role model. What could you possibly teach him that I can't? Catching fish and picking up girls? Some role model you are: at forty you're still here, and your grandest aspiration is to fuck the tourists."

His shining eyes suddenly clouded over, even as he smiled. "We've known each other since birth and you still know nothing about me, Teresa. You don't understand anything."

"Here he is again, the man who understands everything."

"Listen to me, I know I'm the last person who should give advice on how to live. But I think you waste too much energy tearing down the things you love. Love them as they are, because if not, you ruin them. You're always looking for the defects in everything."

"It's that I like being proven wrong. But if I think badly of something, I'm usually right."

"The world is imperfect. We are imperfect. You're too angry, Teresa, you're angry for no real reason. Enjoy this island and your growing son. And if you're in need, I'm here. I'm leaving soon for two weeks. They hired me on a sailing trip in Greece but afterwards I'll be back. I'll come back and bring you a dog from the mainland. What kind of dog do you want? Let's hear it."

"What do you think, since you know me so well and everything about me? What kind of dog do I want?"

"You want a white and orange setter, like Irma."

How annoying that he was right once again. I denied it and told him, "You're wrong. A half-breed is fine, a puppy from the kennel. I don't care for a purebred. It's for Lorenzo, not for me."

27.

I did everything to keep the hotel open for as long as possible, launching a campaign of offers for off-season divers. I had to make sure that even the winter months were not wasted. In reality, at the end of the month, there was almost nothing left, between the costs of heating and staff, despite having reduced them to a minimum. My mom had told me; I thought I knew more than her and, as usual, I was wrong.

At Christmas I decided to stay open, even though there were no reservations. But Red, Nonnalina, and Caterina came to visit. For lunch we prepared cappelletti in broth and it was the first time that Nonnalina was unable to make the pasta with her hands. She was over ninety years old and the time had come for her to receive some of the care that she had always given. It was a forced rest that she tried to rebel against as much as she could, taking half an hour to set the table, clear the table, check that the windows were closed, and dry the sink. She would never get used to unproductive leisure time.

Nonnalina received many gifts: a pearl necklace, a perfume from Paris, a cardigan with golden buttons. Everything made her happy. She gathered the objects carefully, arranging them in small pyramids on the table while Lorenzo, who had ten packages under the tree and only four relatives around him, grumbled in incomprehensible discontent. "These kids have too much, they don't know what to do with it anymore," said the great-grandmother with disappointment. Red began a provocative speech about the generations. I had always liked hearing her talk. I liked when she was still filled with that fervor that put everyone in line. It reminded me how nice it was to hear her deliberate when we were little, how persuasive her speeches on justice were. But in that speech I was the implicit actor in the part about the failed, lazy, passive generation and since Caterina had too many arguments in my defense, I

decided not to intervene except by taking five stacked
glasses from Nonna's hand to bring to the kitchen. A quarrel
began from which I escaped. I joined Lorenzo with Ponzio in
tow, without a leash. The dog had been with us for three
weeks. We accepted that horrible name because Pietro had
brought it from Ponza, where he had gone with a friend who
wanted to buy a sailboat. He said that the owner of the boat
had found a litter behind his garage and asked Pietro if he
could take them. He had replied that the most he could take
was one and, out of the six, he chose the all black one, "to better disguise the racial mix," and thus had saved him. Ponzio
was therefore the chosen one. And he was given that name
because, traditionally, those who are born by a port or on a
boat take its name.

Lorenzo was on our rock. There was a cold wind that
swirled around us. I found a wool cap in my pocket and tried
to put it on him, but he didn't want it. So I wore it. We sat with
the dog between us. I would have really liked a cigarette. I
hugged him; he rested his head on my shoulder.

"Mom, do you know the story about the shepherd sailors?"

"No, what's the story?"

"Pietro told me about it. He said that in ancient times when
the world was almost uninhabited, sailors brought animals
with them and then left them in pairs on the deserted islands
where they stopped along their journey. Two goats, two pigs.
So when they returned, maybe after a few years, they were sure
to find something to eat. Because the animals had reproduced
and there were no predators. The same happened at Giglio.
Cool, no? A great idea."

"The wild farms. The ancient sailors were ingenious."

"Sometimes I wonder if maybe God did the same with
Adam and Eve, and at some point he will return to Earth hungry, and there are more than six billion of us . . ."

"Sometimes I wonder how certain thoughts come to you.

Don't worry. Adam and Eve did not exist, and if the Bible were right, it doesn't say anywhere that God feeds on human flesh."

"Mom, you make me laugh because you respond to these things. You take everything literally."

"I've lost my edge, Lori. I'm missing the second level of interpretation. Strange, because I had it before."

"Maybe because you don't talk with anyone who uses the second level."

"No one, except you."

"I'm eleven."

"So?"

"So nothing."

While he stroked the dog's head and I his, I thought that I should not waste that head, which deserved to travel the world and be close to other heads that knew more, not remain attached to a rock.

On December 30th, Caterina left. When I accompanied her to the ferry in the morning, I had a bout of gastritis of the kind that folds me in two. The port was deserted. After Christmas lunch, we had closed the hotel and would only reopen at the end of February.

I had in front of me an expanse of empty time, which echoed with the space, also deserted, and I myself felt open in the expanses of the cold air that gave me nausea. Many people were leaving. Caterina told me, "Damn, it's even worse than usual. It always seems more and more deserted to me. When we were young it wasn't like this. They all left, they did it. I wonder why you don't."

"I don't have a choice at the moment, Caterina."

"Of course you do, Teresa, don't stop. Do it for Lorenzo. Go around the world ten times. Everything will always be the same here. And you'll always be a mainlander, anyway. We'll keep Giglio for when we're old."

"I'll use these two months to study French," I said without much conviction.

"Great," she said, less convinced than me. She knew the effect of mental laziness that the island created. It was all-engulfing. Looking for words that did not come, I wandered between memories and intentions. There was no need to say more. We hugged for a long time.

In the days that followed New Year's, I asked my mom and Nonna to stay a little longer with us before going back to Orbetello. Not that I needed them to. I didn't have much to do, besides prepare food for Lorenzo, the accounting for the hotel, and some maintenance work. A kind of *horror vacui* came over me, a frightened depression. The darkness that came early in the garden, the sound of the wind that passed through the chimney, and the sea that never stood still scared me. The houses close to ours were vacant in the winter and for the first time in my life, I was uncomfortable being alone with Lorenzo. I felt that I might be unable to protect him.

In hindsight, maybe I was just waiting. And I was right to be afraid of all that darkness.

The darkness that arrived on the night between the 13th and the 14th of January, 2012.

28.

Friday evening, around ten. The grandmothers had left two days earlier, so three of us remained. I'm already in my pajamas, the television is on and the fireplace is lit, an open book in my hand, Ponzio beside me, an empty glass of rum on the table. Lorenzo is in his room with the smartphone he got for Christmas from Red, texting. I'm annoyed by the continuous *beep beep* so I get up to take that thing out of his hands. As I pass the large living-room window I see something other than the usual scary, black landscape. Lights. A thousand lights. In long rows, higher than the dock. Suddenly they go off and on again. My heart leaps into my throat. I scream my son's name.

From the window we see a gigantic and slightly tilted ship passing slowly by the port. Lorenzo arrives with his phone in hand. "Oh my God, what the fuck is that?" He takes a photo but we can't see anything. We hear seven long and deep signals from the ship's siren, and they echo in the calm of the night.

These cruise ships would often pass by in the summer, very close, and they'd blast their horn three times to say hello. This time, however, something must have gone very wrong.

I snatch the phone from Lorenzo. I'm looking for Pietro in his contacts. Meanwhile, the ship begins to turn slowly, the bow points to the port but gradually recedes and rotates counterclockwise. It floats in the dark. It's bigger than anything that could have ever been in that window, enormous, and it's coming towards us. Pietro picks up and says, "Oh God, oh God! Did you see that? Something's going to happen. It's a cruise ship and it's sinking! Get dressed quickly and come down. Let's go see from the dock."

Lorenzo and I keep looking outside, unable to move for an indefinite time, until the lights go out completely and the ship ends its lopsided run with a dull crash that fills the silence of the night, finally beaching itself upon the Gabbianara rock, just outside the port. I run to get dressed, grab my cell phone, call Ettore who is staying at Castello. I apologize, I tell him to go down to the port, to bring Irene and Annamaria as well because there is a cruise ship here in front of us that has been wrecked. He has to come. Help will be needed. I call my mom in Orbetello. "I don't believe it, I don't believe it, how is this possible," she repeats.

The Carabinieri are already at the port, along with the brigade and the commander and crew of the ferry who are preparing to approach the ship. It's almost eleven and its journey seems to be over. Shouts can be heard from the ship. So many screams that they build up and reach the shore. One thing I will never forget. Our night of war begins. The first motorboat arrives, followed by another. There are people crying and screaming. Fifty disembark at a time. They don't know where they are.

"Lorenzo, stay close to me, I don't want to lose sight of you. Let's go open the hotel, turn the heat on, everything. Let's open the rooms, all eighteen, and take the blankets out of the closets. Lorenzo, you have to help me, do you understand?"

He runs behind me, taking photos.

"Don't waste time." Other lifeboats arrive, and a helicopter. There are people in the sea. Many. Suddenly, Lorenzo is no longer behind me. I shout his name with all the strength I have, I see him going back, making his way through the crowd. I turn around too, grab Pietro by the arm, and cry even louder but Pietro tells me, "He's with me. We'll help those arriving, then we'll bring them to you. Don't worry. Run, run Teresa, we can't waste time, go and turn everything on."

Those who jumped overboard arrive and the hotel is the closest shelter. I ring the doorbells of the neighboring houses and ask everyone I know to come and help me, to bring duvets and blankets. There is a group of men patrolling the rocks in front of San Lorenzo with torches. A French couple that swam arrives first. They have injured feet. I put them in Room 1 and explain how to get hot water. I put all the blankets on them. He cries and can't stop and she scolds him. I tell him to calm down, the doctor is coming. I leave them and ask Annamaria to go and look for some clothes. They arrive in groups of three, four, it doesn't stop. They are wet, they are wounded, Italians, Germans, Americans, French, Spanish, in elegant clothes, in synthetic pants, Filipinos and Indians dressed as waiters. Life jackets pile up in one corner, quickly becoming a growing pyramid on the floor, slippery from seawater and blood. I call everyone I can to help me. There's Giuliana, who brings more blankets, collected from house to house, and Laura with the first-aid kit from the infirmary. Irene is at the bar and almost everything is gone. Now there's probably two hundred people in the dining room; the bedrooms are occupied by the wounded and by those with hypothermia or in shock. The wide eyes of the survivors cannot be forgotten, especially those with young children.

On the veranda of the outdoor bar, they laid three bodies, covered with hotel sheets. I see Bazza and Gullo carrying another corpse. I see the ferry returning: it has already dropped off the first load of people on the mainland. We hear sirens and helicopters and rafts arrive with flashing lights. Ettore said that these kinds of ships can hold up to five thousand people. Five thousand people who are all arriving at once—there are around a hundred of us here, and we don't even have space for everyone to stand. Thermal blankets arrive, I don't know from where. Doctors and nurses also arrive. The things from the bar are gone, so I open the kitchen. Franca, our cook, has arrived. She starts cooking pasta because even though it's two in the morning, someone must be hungry. I go to help another ten people who arrive from the rocks. In the lounge, there's a guy wearing a jacket from the ship's company who has a list of names, he's going through the lounge identifying people. I put the new arrivals in Room 4, asking the people who are already there if they can leave, as another ferry is ready to take them away. I hold by the arm a woman in her sixties with redone lips and gold bracelets who asks me to help find her sister. They were together on the ship but the sister wasn't able to get on the same lifeboat as her. I take her to the lounge and stop the gentleman with the list; we're looking for Mariateresa Berli, but she is not yet among the passengers identified on the island. The woman, to whom a boy gives up his seat, bows her head and cries and her lips curl in an unnatural shape as she says, "She doesn't know how to swim, she was afraid, I should have held onto her hand. Why didn't I hold her hand? I always held her hand when we were little." I tell her that if she was behind her, she must have taken the next lifeboat. I beg her to stay there, say that I'll look for her sister and certainly find her. I run into Nanni, the traffic cop, and I ask where I can find someone with an updated list of the surviving passengers. He tells me to try the church. I climb the steps two at a time and get to the churchyard. Before me is a flood of people. It looks like a painting of the Apocalypse. My heart beats too fast. I have to slow down. I call my sister. I know it's the middle of the night but I need to hear her voice. She answers me half asleep. She already knows everything, Mom has already called her. She asks me what's happening and how it's going. Hastily, I tell her, "I love you," and I hang up. I go to look for the woman with the passenger list. Her list also says that Mariateresa Berli has not made it to shore. The pharmacy has been stormed and there is nothing left on the shelves. I go back to the port. Other lifeboats arrive but there is no more space for them to moor. Everyone is screaming. I try to stop the man who has the names of the people who have left for Porto Santo Stefano. He can't pay attention to me because he has to keep track of the next boarding. I grab his arm—tell me if Mariateresa Berli is there. He does not respond. I snatch the list from his hands, he gets pissed, but I scream louder than him. In the end, he checks and tells me that Mariateresa Berli left for Porto Santo Stefano on the ferry an hour ago. I go to find Lorenzo. I can't find him so I try to call him but his phone is off. I run across the pier and a woman, perhaps Russian, asks me if we are in France. I tell her, "Italy, Italy." I see Pietro moor a life raft carrying ten people wearing marathon recovery blankets. I cry to him, "Where is Lorenzo? You told me you'd keep him with you!" He signals for me to wait and doesn't answer until everyone has left the boat. Then he comes to me. He tells me that he sent him to accompany an elderly person to the medic and has not seen him since. "Good. You're reliable." I have to go to the hotel. I tell him to look for Lorenzo and bring him to me. He nods yes and I see blood on his hands.

I'm not worried about my son. It's a feeling that at this moment I cannot afford; he wasn't on the ship. I walk toward the hotel again, passing the many people with whom I share this battlefield. I don't look anyone in the eyes anymore. It's my nemesis, me who admired those who waged war, the Resistance, those who felt History on their own skin, the victims of terrorism. Well, here it is, my own surreal war. It's 2012 and History ended a long time ago around these parts. And yet it comes back, to this unknown rock, like the dusty pin of a grenade in disguise, in the form of this grotesque battle of soldiers bejeweled and dressed up in evening wear, a war in which suffering and death don't come to pass for a great ideal, for a revolution, for liberation, but for the banal carelessness of a mediocre spineless man at the helm of a glittering circus of fake, neon-colored crystals, hydromassage tubs and sports pitches, music lounges and all-inclusive cocktails, chrome handles, slot machines and jewelry shops, parlor games, carpeting and strobe mirrors, waitresses who are also dancers and dishwashers who act as acrobatic bartenders. In this vapid century, one could die even for a cruise called *Scent of citrus fruit*.

I find the older woman with her head resting on the table over her bejeweled arm. Even though she is asleep, I wake her up. It is so nice to be able to tell her that her sister is alive, even if she didn't hold her hand. Her fake lip trembles. We hug. I tell her that I'll bring her to the next ferry. She asks me what my name is and I tell her, "Teresa, like your younger sister." "Older sister," she specifies.

As I'm leaving, I see Pietro and Lorenzo arrive. I ask Pietro to take the woman to the ferry and I hurry back to my son. He has spirited eyes and it seems impossible to me that he didn't cry, that he wasn't afraid, that he hadn't looked for me all night. Now I have proof of his extraordinary strength.

"I can't believe what I saw, Mom."

"Incredible, Lori. I know. I also feel that I've seen things that are impossible to even imagine. A disaster like this simply could not have happened."

"I also took videos."

"Okay Lori, but now please, without making a scene, go home and go to bed. It's after four and you did everything you could have done. You're my little hero."

He gives me a kiss and tells me, "You know Mom, maybe this is punishment for when I said that nothing ever happens during the winter in Giglio."

"What self-centeredness."

"Ah, you fell for it again. You take everything so literally."

"Lorenzo, come on, this isn't funny."

"I know, that's why I did it. To make you smile. You're almost scary with that face and red eyes."

"Really?"

"Yes, but everyone looks that way . . . Mom, did you know that the captain left the ship before the others?"

"How do you know?"

"Pietro showed me two hours ago. He told me that he would have rather shot himself in the head."

"A real captain couldn't do anything else. But a real sailor wouldn't end up in such a mess."

"You're right. I'm going. But in a little while, you should come too."

Pietro returns with the task of bringing people from the hotel to the ferry in groups of twenty. We try to cover everyone, but there are no more blankets. We use the white tablecloths and the runners that we put on the tables at breakfast.

It's almost six when the lobby empties. The sun is rising above our disaster. The sky slowly turns from purple to yellow like a large bruise. What the night had hidden now appears in all its enormity. There is a gigantic prow, like a white mountain, that stands out in the foreground of the corner of *my* window and now occupies *my* oldest childhood memory: the view from *my* rock. This ship has irreversibly violated something sacred: a landscape of granite and sea, unchanged for five million years. Who could have foreseen that something could change that corner of the world where only a few seagulls rest their feet every so often?

29.

Pietro had arrived with wounded hands and a pallor that he'd never worn before, against which dark purple under-eye bags stood out. It was 6:30 A.M.

"Listen, can I come to your house?"

". . ."

"I can't be alone. I don't think I could sleep."

"But I'm not going home. There are things to do here. The journalists have already arrived."

"You need to sleep too."

"I can't."

"Let's go." He gave me his jacket and we walked home. The jacket smelled of sea and sweat. I felt the nausea rising. When we got home, I laid down on the couch. Even from there I could see the windows, I could see the wreck in the mirror that my father had hung on the wall of the dining room so that diners who had their backs to the sea could still enjoy the view. In the middle of the floor there was a liquid stain. Ponzio must have pissed himself. I couldn't get up to clean. The telephone rang in my pocket but Pietro grabbed it and turned it off. He went upstairs and I heard him enter the bathroom. I saw him return with some paper towels which he laid on the dog piss.

He said to me, "Lorenzo is sound asleep in bed," and I was amazed that I hadn't thought to check. Then he laid down next to me and we fell asleep right there, on the couch that was too narrow for the two of us.

Red and Nonnalina had taken an early ferry to come and help. When they arrived, they found us still in that position, asleep in the full morning light. I heard my grandmother say in dialect, "Who is that?" I sat up with a half scream, choked by fright. I went to turn on the coffee machine; Pietro said hello and that he was just leaving. I recounted the night to Mom, tried unsuccessfully to fall asleep again, took a very long shower, and went out.

Wherever I walked, from whatever perspective, the wreck was there, in the foreground. To avoid it, the only option was to turn your back and not look at the sea. The port itself was an unrecognizable anthill of people, boats, tents of all kinds of corps—the Carabinieri, divers, firefighters, spelunkers, journalists, and vans with parabolic antennae for international television. The world had come to Giglio and we were not prepared at all. I thought to myself, this three-hundred-meter-long ship, full of diesel fuel and supplies because it had just departed, which has more things inside it than Giglio has ever seen, with its five thousand beds, thirteen restaurants, three clubs and arcades: what do we do with this stuff, how do we get rid of it? With my head down, I walked briskly to Pietro's house.

And there, as if we had nothing else to do, as if neither of us could conceive of another plan, like talking about the shipwreck, crying together, or preparing coffee, we undressed and made love. With even more anger than we had when we were sixteen, mixed with the nostalgia that we had repressed for years. To meet again his hands, his salty taste, all that strength that I never found in anyone else. And me, his mold. And to finally come, which was the wrong verb because it was a finding again, after such a long wait, home.

At lunchtime I went to the hotel. The cook had already served the second round of pasta for the divers and the Carabinieri. My mom updated me, "All the rooms are rented for the next ten days, half of them by law enforcement, the other half by journalists or people from the coast guard." She was exhausted so I sent her home. Nonnalina kept still in a corner of the room, sitting in front of the wreck to watch, as if she needed all that time to chew, swallow, and digest the image. I understood. I went to her, she asked me how many were dead. I told her about thirty and that some were missing. "Poor people, poor people." Yes, Nonna, the poor people.

Lorenzo came running. "You won't believe it, Mom. I put a video on YouTube that I took last night. In two hours it got more than twenty thousand views. From all over the world."

"What did you do? Are you crazy?"

"What, Mom? It's a testimony."

"Lorenzo, I don't want you to put your stuff on the Internet. I've told you a thousand times. I don't like it, take it down right away."

"Mom, at least watch it."

He handed me his phone. I pressed play. There was his voice, commenting over dark footage of a lifeboat approaching. His voice seemed to belong to a child even younger than him as he said: tonight there was a shipwreck on the island of Giglio. A cruise ship came too close and crashed on the rocks. Now it's stopped, all tipped over near Porto. Luckily, it did not sink. The first lifeboats with passengers on board are arriving. Here they are.

In the video, the lifeboat banged into the dock. A dozen women in vests got out, followed by four waiters, two of whom were holding an enormous bag, the kind with metal handles, and they carried it away, running. The images were shaky, but the voice was clear: "Here, some people from the shipwreck are getting off, and that heavy thing that they were carrying was a bag full of money. It must have been a hundred kilos of euros. They're bringing it to safety. Understand? Instead of the passengers, they loaded the money, not later, not last, but first. Isn't it strange that it matters more than the people?"

The commentary ended. The video resumed with another lifeboat approaching and then his sneakers walking, recording frantic voices in foreign languages, and then stopped.

"Lorenzo, this is important documentation, but I want you to take it off of YouTube. You're just a child. You probably had to lie about your age to put it online."

"Why do you want me to take it down? Everyone is watching my video!"

"Exactly, because everyone is watching it. That's not okay. You're eleven years old, understand? I don't want you to expose yourself like that. Look, people are commenting, they're writing bad words and insults, it's not okay. Come here, because we're removing it immediately," I said to him, gesturing to my computer.

"No. No, Mom. Why do you have to censor me? It's an important thing that I did. I witnessed a historical event and I saw something that other people should know about."

"Who said they need to know, huh? So now you're a journalist, a sociologist—what else do you know at the wise age of eleven? I said we're taking it down and that's that. If you don't tell me how to do it, I'll ask the cyber police, I'll say you're a minor, and it won't be hard to prove since I'm your mother. But if you save me the time of reporting it, we'll all be happier."

He tinkered around on my computer for a few minutes with his jaw clenched, then showed me that the content was no longer available.

"Good job," I told him. "Maybe in a while, when things have calmed down a bit, you can put it back up. Now we have to try not to throw fuel on the fire, understand? We helped so many people, and you did so well, so to say that they saved the money before the passengers is wrong, it sounds like an accusation. Let's stay out of it, please. Now what we have to try and do is save our island from this disaster, so there's no point in twisting the knife. Do you agree, sweetheart?"

"No, not at all. Sweetheart my ass. These people do disgusting things: they think they own the sea with these shitty transatlantic ships, they come close even though they don't know how to properly, but nobody says anything, until they crash on the rocks, people die in the sea, and they fill the lifeboats with casino money. And we Gigliesi are fine with it because we're the heroes in this situation. We're the good guys, right, Mom? Like you, always good. So good. Especially with me."

He ran off. The thing that struck me most from his harangue was that he had said "we Gigliesi," first person plural, including himself in the group. As for the rest, it was pure Lorenzo: he listened to the arguments adults made and repeated them if he agreed with them but with the useless reasoning of a child. The truth without humility.

But in any case it was too late. Ten minutes later, a journalist from a cable news channel arrived at the hotel and asked me if it was my son who had posted that video on YouTube and if she could interview him. I told her that the video was no longer available, that I would never sign the release, and I really had a lot to do.

Night fell again, without being able to turn off anything with its darkness. Another journalist called me at the hotel to ask about my son and the video, but I told him no, it wasn't my son and that I didn't know anything about the clips or children.

I started setting the tables in the dining room.

We had asked everyone to be on time at 8:30 P.M. because dinner would only be served once and there was one menu.

It was completely full, groups of men only, waxed work

boots, cellphones in hand, diving equipment without the usual overtones of fun. All they did was talk about the incident and expound upon details, certain dynamics, schedules, routes, and knot speed; everyone claimed to know how it had gotten to the Scole rocks the night before, what the captain was doing and why. At the end of the shift, after Annamaria served coffee, it was our turn. At our silent table, Lorenzo sulked, Nonnalina was in her acoustic isolation, and Elena was exhausted. The television was always on, showing the images that I could see from the window.

I had never experienced days anything like those in my life. A trauma caused by an impossible event, a rediscovered love, all together, enough emotions for an entire lifetime all concentrated in a few hours.

At a certain point, on the TV, played an amateur recording that I recognized. Red turned up the volume and we could hear Lorenzo's voice; it was subtitled, and the video ended on his shoes. Then he was there, with the green lighthouse in the background, lights on his face—they must have recorded it an hour earlier—there he was, my son, already named the little hero of Giglio, repeating his speech against the cruiseliners, the same one he had given me a few hours ago.

I slapped my hand on the table. "Christ! I guess what I say doesn't matter at all!" but in the meantime applause had already started in the dining room, someone had gotten up to shake hands with Lorenzo, who blushed but didn't shy away from collecting his laurels. My mother said, "Teresa, it's my fault, don't blame him, I signed the release. It was the right thing to do, damn it, and what he had to say is crucial! These new generations are more combative than us, they have more weapons, they are stronger. Did you see the video he made? Your son witnessed a unique event, Teresa, and he showed how this event was the result of a distorted society controlled by money above all else. Do you understand the gravity of what he said? Lorenzo is a child with ideals a thousand times stronger than yours: how can you think that it's okay to censor him?"

"Mom, he's eleven, he's like all children, and you're just like all the other nonnas who are easily persuaded by their grandsons' sweet-talking. Whatever happens to Lorenzo now will be your fault. And as for the journalists, you can deal with them. He won't be on television again. Until proven otherwise, I have parental authority."

"Of course I take responsibility for what I did: have you ever known me to avoid it? Maybe Lorenzo has a future in politics, and it definitely won't be thanks to the fact that you clip his wings and repeatedly tell him to behave."

"A future in politics! A future in politics! What am I hearing? Do I have to remind you that he's a child, Mom? Just a child!"

"He's a child who at eleven years old has more strength and ideals than you at forty."

I had lost to her once more. I had lost against both of them, but it didn't hurt. It's true, the people around me were stronger, they were capable of making decisions, to carry on their battles, they were protagonists. Not me. But now I knew that I couldn't force my role, that the things I could do were all right there, that I could count on my resilience and love them.

Caterina called me: she had seen the report from Paris and wanted to talk to Lorenzo, but first she asked me, "Now what will you do?" I replied, "I'll be here, Cate, I'll be here as long as I'm needed."

And I thought that response really meant a lot more, that I would stay to guard and protect our home. To love the things that I had always loved just as they are. Including a boy that I'd wanted to forget. And with whom I could now see doing anything with, going away, or staying here forever. Letting him be a father to my son. Meanwhile, we would wait for the day that the ship would leave, we would fight for it to leave no trace of itself, and that day, when our rock would look like it had before, would be our liberation.

Here he was, Pietro, arriving at the right moment. Without giving him time to reach the table and say hello, I headed towards him, grabbing my coat and scarf. Without saying anything, we went to the big rock. The divers continued their shifts searching around the wreck for any other missing people.

We stood side by side and he said, "There's nowhere left in the world. Not a single fucking place in this sad, shitty world. I thought that Giglio had been spared, and instead, look." I nodded and didn't say anything. The view that had always brought me so much happiness now caused indescribable pain, but at the same time, it opened my eyes to how much I loved my island and what I was willing to do to defend it. I watched Pietro as he rolled a cigarette. I tried closing my eyes for a few seconds. When I reopened them, everything was still there, the rock, the ship lying on its side, Pietro with his enormous blue jacket. But something had changed forever. The ring that bound me to my childhood had broken. The nostalgia, the boat with Vittorio, the races on the beach with Caterina and Irma, Red in the Italian Communist Party headquarters, swimming in the middle of the night, it had all been crushed by a ship that weighed thousands of tons.

I knew that I was there and that I couldn't do anything else but look forward. I squeezed Pietro's free hand in his pocket. Suddenly, the wind picked up.